WORLD FAMOUS TRIALS

PUSTAK MAHAL®

J-3/16 , Daryaganj, New Delhi-110002
☎ 23276539, 23272783, 23272784 • *Fax:* 011-23260518
E-mail: info@pustakmahal.com • *Website:* www.pustakmahal.com

Sales Centre

- 10-B, Netaji Subhash Marg, Daryaganj, New Delhi-110002
  ☎ 23268292, 23268293, 23279900 • *Fax:* 011-23280567
  E-mail: rapidexdelhi@indiatimes.com
- 6686, Khari Baoli, Delhi-110006
  ☎ 23944314, 23911979

Branches

Bengaluru: ☎ 080-22234025 • *Telefax:* 080-22240209
E-mail: pustak@airtelmail.in • pustak@sancharnet.in
Mumbai: ☎ 022-22010941, 022-22053387
E-mail: rapidex@bom5.vsnl.net.in
Patna: ☎ 0612-3294193 • *Telefax:* 0612-2302719
E-mail: rapidexptn@rediffmail.com
Hyderabad: *Telefax:* 040-24737290
E-mail: pustakmahalhyd@yahoo.co.in

ISBN 978-81-223-1271-3

Edition: 2012

Printed at : Param Offsetters, Okhla, New Delhi-110020

Contents

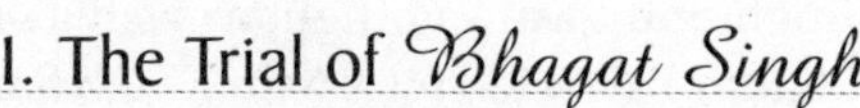

1. The Trial of Bhagat Singh

Bhagat Singh was an Indian freedom fighter considered to be one of the most influential revolutionaries of the Indian independence movement. He is often referred to as *Shaheed* Bhagat Singh, the word *Shaheed* meaning "martyr".

Early Life

Bhagat Singh was born to Kishan Singh Sandhu and Vidyavati Kaur at Chak No. 105 village in the Lyallpur district of the Punjab Province in British India. He came from a patriotic Jat Sikh family, some of whom had participated in movements supporting the independence of India and others had served in Maharaja Ranjit Singh's army. His ancestors came from the Khatkar Kalan village near the town of Banga in Nawanshahr district which is now renamed as *Shaheed* Bhagat Singh Nagar, Punjab. He was nicknamed *Bhaganwala* by his grandmother, meaning *the lucky one* since the news of the release of his uncle Ajit

Singh from Mandlay Jail and his father Kishan Singh from Lahore Jail coincided with his birth. His grandfather, Arjun Singh, was a follower of Swami Dayananda Saraswati's Hindu reformist movement, Arya Samaj, which had a considerable influence on Singh. His uncles, Ajit Singh and Swaran Singh, as well as his father, were members of the Ghadar Party, led by Kartar Singh Sarabha Grewal and Har Dayal. Ajit Singh was forced to flee to Persia because of pending cases against him while Swaran Singh died in 1910 at his home after releasing from Borstal Jail, Lahore.

Unlike many Sikhs of his age, Bhagat Singh did not attend Khalsa High School in Lahore because his grandfather did not approve of the school officials' loyalism to the British authorities. Instead, his father enrolled him in Dayanand Anglo Vedic High School, an Arya Samaj school. In 1919, the Jallianwala Bagh massacre made him think about India's independence. In 1920, at the age of 13, Singh began to follow Mahatma Gandhi's Non-Cooperation Movement. At this point, he openly defied the and followed Gandhi's wishes by burning his government school books and any imported clothing. Following Gandhi's withdrawal of the movement after the violent murders of policemen by villagers from Chauri Chaura, Uttar Pradesh in 1922, Singh, disgruntled with Gandhi's non–violent action, joined the Young Revolutionary Movement and began advocating a violent movement against the British.

He was 14 when, on February 20, 1921, the custodian of Nankana Sahib (the birthplace of Guru Nanak) and his men, fired on Akali protesters. The firing was widely condemned, and an agitation was launched till the control of the historic gurudwara was restored to the Sikhs. This incident left a deep impact on him.

In 1923, Singh joined National College, Lahore, where he made a positive impression, academically. He was also a member of the college dramatics society. He was fluent in Urdu, Hindi, Punjabi, English, and Sanskrit. In 1923, Singh won an essay competition organised by the Punjab Hindi Sahitya Sammelan. His essay, *Punjab's Language and Script*, quoted Punjabi literature and discussed the problems of the Punjab, and were way ahead of his age. This grabbed the attention of members of the Punjab Hindi Sahitya Sammelan including its General Secretary Professor Bhim Sen Vidyalankar. He became a member of the organisation Naujawan Bharat Sabha

(Youth Society of India). In the Naujawan Bharat Sabha, Singh and his fellow revolutionaries grew popular amongst the youth. He joined the Hindustan Republican Association, which had prominent leaders like Ram Prasad Bismil, Chandrashekhar Azad and Ashfaqulla Khan. A year later, on being pressurised by his family to get married, Singh left his house in Lahore and went to Kanpur. In a note left behind for his father, Singh said: "My life has been dedicated to the noblest cause, that of the freedom of the country. Therefore, there is no rest or worldly desire that can lure me now..." It is also believed that he went to Kanpur to attempt freeing the Kakori train robbery prisoners from jail, but returned to Lahore for unknown reasons. On the day of Dussehra in October 1926, a bomb exploded in Lahore. Singh was arrested for his alleged involvement in this Dussehra Bomb Case on May 29, 1927, but was let off for good behaviour against a heavy security of Rs 60,000, after about five weeks of his arrest. He wrote for and edited Urdu and Punjabi newspapers published from Amritsar. In September 1928, a meeting of various revolutionaries from across India was called at Delhi under the banner of the Kirti Kisan Party (Workers and Peasants Party). Singh was the secretary of the meet. His later revolutionary activities were carried out as a leader of this association.

LATER REVOLUTIONARY ACTIVITIES

Lala Lajpat Rai's Death and the Saunders' Murder

The British government created a commission under Sir John Simon to report on the current political situation in India in 1928. The Indian political parties boycotted the commission because it did not include a single Indian in its membership and it was met with protests all over the country. When the commission visited Lahore on October 30, 1928, Lala Lajpat Rai led a non-violent protest against the commission in a silent march, but the police responded with violence. The Lahore Superintendent of Police, James A. Scott, ordered the police lathi charge against the non-violent protesters and personally assaulted Lajpat Rai, who was grievously injured. When Rai died less than three weeks later, it was widely assumed that Scott's blows had hastened his demise. Singh vowed to take revenge. He joined other revolutionaries, Shivaram Rajguru, Sukhdev Thapar, Jai Gopal and Chandrashekhar Azad, in a plot to kill Scott. Jai Gopal was supposed to identify the chief and signal Singh to shoot. However, in a case of mistaken identity, Gopal signalled Singh on the appearance of John P. Saunders, an Assistant Superintendent of Police. He was shot by Rajguru and Singh while leaving the District Police Headquarters at about 4:15 p.m. on December 17, 1928. Head Constable Chanan Singh was also killed when he came to Saunders' aid.

Dramatic Escape

After killing Saunders, they escaped through the D.A.V. College entrance, on the other side of the road. Head Constable Chanan Singh who chased them was fatally injured by Chandrashekhar Azad's covering fire. They then fled on bicycles to the prearranged places of safety. The police launched a massive search operation to catch the culprits and blocked all exits and entrances. The police sealed all roads from the city; the CID kept a watch at the railway stations and all young men leaving Lahore were scrutinised. They hid themselves for the next two days. Sukhdev called on Durga Devi Vohra on December 19, 1928 and she agreed to help them. They decided to catch the train departing from Lahore for Howrah en route Bathinda early the next morning. That train was chosen so that they could escape before the arrival of the CID picket. Singh, in Western attire carrying the sleeping infant; Durga, in her most impressive attire; and Rajguru shuffling under luggage, left the house at about 5 a.m. On reaching the station, Singh keeping his facial profile reasonably covered on one side with a slightly raised collar of the overcoat and on the other by the sleeping infant, purchased two tickets, a joint second class Christmas return ticket and a third class one for the servant, for Cawnpore. They walked side by side into the railway station with Rajguru carrying the luggage behind in a servile manner. Both men carried loaded revolvers with them in case of an untoward incident. As a respectable young couple with a child, dressed in Western style clothing and holding a joint second class Christmas return ticket, they avoided police attention. Singh and Rajguru boarded the train without causing any suspicion. To avoid recognition, Singh had shaved off his beard and cut his hair. Breaking journey at Cawnpore they went to Lucknow, as the CID at Howrah kept a close watch on passengers coming directly from Lahore. At Lucknow, Rajguru left separately for Varanasi. Singh, Durga Devi and the infant went to Howrah. Durga Devi returned to Lahore a few days later.

Bombs in the Assembly

In the face of actions by the revolutionaries, the British government enacted the Defence of India Act to give more power to the police. The purpose of the Act was to combat revolutionaries like Singh. In response to this Act, the Hindustan Socialist Republican Association planned to explode a bomb in the Central Legislative Assembly where the ordinance was going to be passed. This idea was originated by Singh, who was influenced by a similar bombing by a martyr anarchist Auguste Vaillant in the French Assembly. It was decided that Singh should go to Russia, while Batukeshwar Dutt should carry on the bombing with Sukhdev. Sukhdev then forced Singh to call for another meeting and there it was decided, against the initial agreement, that Batukeshwar Dutt and Singh would carry on the bombing. Singh also disapproved that the two should be escorted after the bombing by the rest of the party.

On April 8, 1929, Singh and Dutt threw two bombs onto the assembly and shouted "*Inquilab Zindabad!*" ("Long Live the Revolution!"). This was followed by a shower of leaflets stating that it takes a loud noise to make the deaf hear. The bombs did not kill anyone; Singh and Dutt claimed that this was deliberate on their part, a claim substantiated both by British forensics investigators who found that the bombs were not powerful enough to cause injury, and by the fact that the bombs were thrown away from people. Singh and Dutt gave themselves up for arrest after the bombing. They intended to use their court appearances as a forum for revolutionary propaganda to advocate the revolutionaries' point of view and, in the process, rekindle patriotic sentiments in the hearts of the people. Singh surrendered his automatic pistol, the same one he had used to pump bullets into Saunders' body, knowing fully well that the pistol would be the highest proof of his involvement in the Saunders' case.

On April 15, 1929, the 'Lahore Bomb Factory' was discovered by the Lahore police, and the other members of HSRA were arrested, out of which seven turned informants, helping the police to connect Singh to the murder of Saunders. Singh, Rajguru, and Sukhdev were charged with the murder. Singh decided to use the court as a tool to publicise his cause for the independence of India. Singh was charged with attempt to murder under section 307 of the Indian Penal Code. Asaf Ali, a member of the Congress Party was his lawyer. The trial started on

May 7, 1929. The Crown was represented by the public prosecutor Rai Bahadur Suryanarayan and the trial magistrate was a British Judge, P.B. Pool. The prosecution's star witness was Sergeant Terry who said that a pistol had been found when he was arrested in the Assembly. This was not factually correct because Singh had himself surrendered the pistol while asking the police to arrest him. Even the eleven witnesses who said that they had seen the two throwing the bombs seemed to have been tutored. The entire incident had been so sudden that nobody could have anticipated it. The magistrate committed both of them to the Sessions Court of Judge Leonard Middleton. Judge Middleton ruled that he had no doubt that the defendant's acts were deliberate and rejected the plea that the bombs were deliberately low–intensity bombs since the impact of the explosion had shattered the wood of one and a half inch thickness in the Assembly. The two were persuaded to file an appeal which was rejected and they were sentenced to transportation for life (fourteen years).

TRIAL AND EXECUTION

Hunger Strike and Lahore Conspiracy Case

The police had gathered substantial evidence against Singh and he was charged with involvement in the killings of Saunders and Head Constable Chanan Singh. The authorities had collected nearly 600 witnesses to establish their charges, which included his colleagues, Jai Gopal and Hans Raj Vohra turning government approvers. Singh was re-arrested for the murder of Saunders and the life imprisonment sentence was kept in abeyance till the outcome of the murder trial.

Singh was sent to Mianwali Jail and B. Dutt to Borstal Jail in Lahore. On reaching Mianwali jail, Singh found that European prisoners got better accommodation, food and daily use items compared to Indian prisoners. While in jail, Singh and other prisoners launched a hunger strike advocating for the rights of prisoners and those facing trial. The aims in their strike were to ensure a decent standard of food for political prisoners, the availability of books and a daily newspaper, as well as better clothing and the supply of toiletry necessities and other hygienic necessities. He also demanded that political prisoners should not be forced to do any labour or undignified work.

As the fast progressed without any solution in sight, Jawaharlal Nehru met Singh and the other protesters. He said:

"I am very much pained to see the distress of the heroes. They have staked their lives in this struggle. They want that political prisoners should be treated as political prisoners. I am quite hopeful that their sacrifice would be crowned with success."

Muhammad Ali Jinnah, one of the politicians present when the Central Legislative Assembly was bombed, made no secret of his sympathies for the Lahore prisoners—commenting on the hunger strike he said:

"The man who goes on hunger strike has a soul. He is moved by that soul, and he believes in the justice of his cause...however much you deplore them and however much you say they are misguided, it is the system, this damnable system of governance, which is resented by the people."

The Government tried several tricks to break the strike. They placed dishes of different types of food in the prison cells to test the resolve of the strikers. Water pitchers were filled with milk so that either the prisoners remained thirsty or broke their strike. But nobody faltered. The authorities attempted forced-feeding, but were resisted. One of the prisoners, Kasuri, swallowed red pepper and drank hot water to clog the feeding tube. The Governor came down from Shimla to meet the jail authorities. But there was no breakthrough.

When the Government realised that this fast had riveted the attention of the people throughout the country, it decided to hurry up the trial, which came to known as the *Lahore Conspiracy Case*. This trial started in Borstal Jail, Lahore, on July 10, 1929. Rai Sahib Pandit Sri Kishen, a first class magistrate, was the judge for this trial. Singh and twenty-seven others were charged with murder, conspiracy and wagering war against the King. A handcuffed Singh, still on hunger strike, had to be brought to the court in a stretcher and his weight had fallen by 14 pounds, from 133 to 119. By then, the condition of Jatindra Nath Das, who was lodged in the same jail and was also on hunger strike, had deteriorated considerably. The jail committee recommended his unconditional release, but the government rejected the suggestion and offered to release him on bail. Jatin died on September 13, 1929. His fast lasted 63 days. After his death, the Viceroy informed London:

"Jatin Das of the Conspiracy Case, who was on hunger strike, died this afternoon at 1 p.m. Last night, five of the hunger strikers gave up their hunger strike. So there are only Bhagat Singh and Dutt who are on strike."

The highest tributes were paid by almost every leader in the country. Mohammad Alam and Gopi Chand Bhargava resigned from the Punjab Legislative Council in protest. Motilal Nehru proposed the adjournment of the Central Assembly as a censure against the inhumanity of the Lahore prisoners. The censure motion was carried by 55 votes against 47.

The Jail Committee requested him to give up his hunger strike and finally it was his father who had his way, armed with a resolution from the Congress party urging them to give up their strike; and it was on the 116th day of their fast, on October 5, 1929 that Singh and Dutt gave up their strike (surpassing the 97 day world record for hunger strikes which was set by an Irish revolutionary). During this hunger strike that lasted 116 days and ended with the British succumbing to his wishes, he gained much popularity among the common Indians. Before the strike his popularity was limited mainly to the Punjab region.

Singh started refocusing on his trial. The crown was represented by the government advocate C.H.Carden–Noad and was assisted by Kalandar Ali Khan, Gopal Lal, and Bakshi Dina Nath who was the prosecuting inspector. The accused were defended by eight different lawyers. When Jai Gopal turned approver, Verma, the youngest of the accused, hurled a slipper at him. The case was ordered to be carried out without the accused or the members of the HSRA present in the court. This created an uproar amongst Singh's supporters as he could no longer publicise his views.

Special Tribunal

The case proceeded at a snail's pace. On May 1, 1930, by declaring an emergency, the Viceroy, Lord Irwin, promulgated an Ordinance to set up a tribunal to try this case. This Special Tribunal was given the power to proceed with the case in the absence of the accused and accept death of the persons giving evidence as a benefit to the defence. The Ordinance, *Lahore Conspiracy Case Ordinance No.3 of 1930*, was to put an end to the proceedings pending in the magistrate's court. The case was transferred from the court of Rai Sahib Pandit Sri Kishan to a Special Tribunal of three high court judges without any right to appeal, except to the Privy Council. The Tribunal comprised – Justice J. Coldstream (president), Justice G. C. Hilton and Justice Agha Hyder (members).

The case opened on May 5, 1930 in the stately Poonch House. On June 20, 1930, the constitution of the Special Tribunal was changed to Justice G. C. Hilton (president), Justice Tapp and Justice Sir Abdul Qadir. On July 2, 1930, a *habeas corpus* petition was filed in the High Court challenging the very constitution of the tribunal and said that it was illegal *ultra vires*. According to the petition, the Viceroy did not have the power to cut short the normal legal procedure. The Government of India Act, 1915, authorised the Viceroy to promulgate an Ordinance to set up a tribunal but only when the situation demanded whereas there was no breakdown in the law and order situation. The petition was however, dismissed as premature. Carden–Noad, the government advocate elaborated the charges which included dacoities, robbing money from banks and the collection of arms and ammunition. The evidence of G.T. Hamilton Harding, Senior Superintendent of Police, took the court by surprise, as he said that he had filed the FIR against the accused under the instructions of the chief secretary to the government of Punjab and he did not know the facts of the case. There were five approvers in total out of which Jai Gopal, Hans Raj Vohra and P.N. Ghosh had been associated with the HRSA for a long time. It was on their stories that the prosecution relied. On July 10, 1930, it issued an order, and copies of the charges framed were served on the fifteen accused in jail, together with copies of an order intimating them that their pleas would be taken on the charges the following day. This trial was a long one, beginning on May 5, 1930, and ending on September 10, 1930. The tribunal framed charges against fifteen out of the eighteen accused. The case against B.K. Dutt was withdrawn as he had already been sentenced to transportation for life in the Assembly Bomb Case.

On October 7, 1930, about three weeks before the expiry of its term, the tribunal delivered its judgement, sentencing Singh, Sukhdev and Rajguru to death by hanging. Others were sentenced to transportation for life and rigorous imprisonment. This judgement was a 300–page one which went into the details of the evidence and said that Singh's participation in the Saunders' murder was the most serious and important fact proved against him and it was fully established by evidence. The warrants for the three were marked with a black border.

Appeal to the Privy Council

A defence committee was constituted in Punjab to file an appeal to the Privy Council against the sentence. Singh did not favour the appeal but his only satisfaction was that the appeal would draw the attention of people in England to the existence of the HSRA. In the case of Bhagat Singh vs. The King Emperor, the points raised by the appellant was that the ordinance promulgated to constitute a special tribunal for the trial was invalid. The government argued that Section 72 of the Government of India Act, 1915 gave the Governor–general unlimited powers to set up a tribunal. Judge Viscount Dunedin who read the judgment dismissed the appeal.

Reactions to the Judgement

After the rejection of the appeal to the Privy Council, Madan Mohan Malviya filed a mercy appeal before the Viceroy on February 14, 1931. The undertrials of the Chittagong Armoury Raid Case sent an appeal to Gandhi to intervene. In his notes dated March 19, 1931, Lord Irwin, the Viceroy of India, recorded in the file:

"While returning Gandhiji asked me if he could talk about the case of Bhagat Singh, because newspapers had come out with the news of his slated hanging on March 24th. It would be a very unfortunate day because on that day the new President of the Congress had to reach Karachi and there would be a lot of hot discussion. I explained to him that I had given a very careful thought to it but I did not find any basis to convince myself to commute the sentence. It appeared he found my reasoning weighty."

The Communist Party of England expressed its reaction to the case:

"The history of this case, of which we do not come across any example in relation to the political cases, reflects the symptoms of callousness and cruelty which is the outcome of bloated desire of the imperialist government of Britain so that fear can be instilled in the hearts of the repressed people."

An abortive plan had been made to rescue Singh and fellow inmates of HSRA from the jail, for the purpose of which Bhagwati Charan Vohra made bombs, but died making them as they exploded accidentally.

Prison Diary

Singh also maintained the use of a diary, in which he eventually wrote 404 pages. In this diary, he made numerous notes relating to the quotations and popular sayings of various people whose views he supported. Prominent in his diary were the views of Karl Marx and Friedrich Engels. The comments in his diary led to an understanding of the philosophical thinking of Singh. While in the condemned cell, he also wrote a pamphlet entitled "Why I am an Atheist", as he was being accused of vanity by not accepting God in the face of death. It is also said that he signed a mercy petition through a comrade Bijoy Kumar Sinha on March 8, 1931.

Execution

Singh, Rajguru and Sukhdev were sentenced to death in the Lahore conspiracy case and ordered to be hanged on March 24, 1931. On March 23, 1931 at 7:30 p.m., Singh was hanged in Lahore Jail with his fellow comrades Rajguru and Sukhdev. The Superintendent of Police (political) Criminal Investigation Department, Punjab, at the time, wrote in his memoirs on "The Saunders Murder Case":

"Normally execution took place at 8 a.m., but it was decided to act at once before the public could become aware of what had happened. At about 7 p.m. shouts of *Inquilab Zindabad* were heard from inside the jail. This was correctly, interpreted as a signal that the final curtain was about to drop."

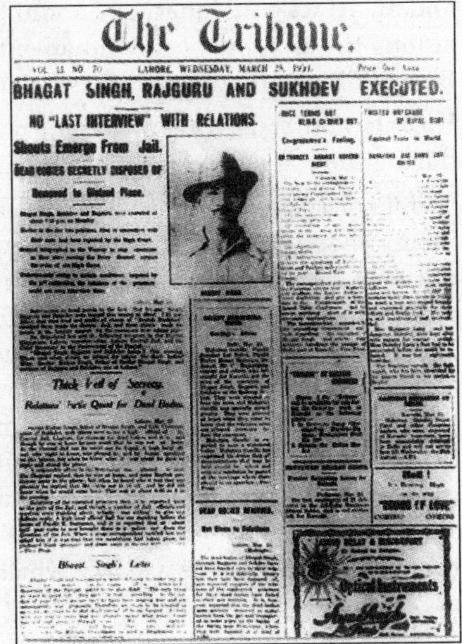

The Tribune.

LAHORE, WEDNESDAY, MARCH

BHAGAT SINGH, RAJGURU AND SUKHDEV EXECUTED.

NO "LAST INTERVIEW" WITH RELATIONS.

Shouts Emerge From Jail.

Thick Veil of Secrecy.

The jail authorities then broke the rear wall of the jail and secretly cremated the three martyrs under cover of darkness outside Ganda Singh Wala village, and then threw the bodies in the Sutlej, about 60 km from Lahore.

Criticism of the Special Tribunal

Singh's trial is an important event in the Indian history because it defied the fundamental doctrine of criminal jurisprudence. The trial was held ex parte in breach of the principles of natural justice according to which no man shall be condemned unless he is given a hearing. The Special Tribunal was a departure from the normal procedure adopted for a trial. There was no appeal except to the Privy Council located in England. The accused were absent from the court and the judgement was passed ex parte. This ordinance was never approved by the Central Assembly or the British Parliament, and it lapsed later without any legal or constitutional sanctity. From the lower court to the tribunal to the Privy Council, it was a preordained judgement in flagrant violation of all tenets of natural justice and a fair and free trial.

Reactions to the execution

The execution of Singh, Rajguru and Sukhdev were reported widely by the press, especially as they were on the eve of the annual convention of the Congress party at Karachi. The New York Times reported:

"A reign of terror in the city of Cawnpore in the United Provinces and an attack on Mahatma Gandhi by a youth outside Karachi were among the answers of the Indian extremists today to the hanging of Bhagat Singh and two fellow assassins."

Hartals and strikes of mourning were called. The Congress party, during the Karachi session, declared:

"While dissociating itself from and disapproving of political violence in any shape or form, this Congress places on record its admiration of the bravery and sacrifice of Bhagat Singh, Sukh Dev and Raj Guru and mourns with their bereaved families the loss of these lives. The Congress is of the opinion that their triple execution was an act of wanton vengeance and a deliberate flouting of the unanimous demand of the nation for commutation. This Congress is further of the opinion that the British Government lost a golden opportunity for promoting good will between the two nations, admittedly held to be crucial at this juncture, and for winning over the methods of peace a party which, driven to despair, resorts to political violence."

Bhagat Singh

Born: September 28, 1907

Died: March 23, 1931

An Indian revolutionary, considered to be one of the most famous martyrs of the Indian freedom struggle.

Born into a Jat Sikh family which had earlier been involved in revolutionary activities against the British Raj, as a teenager Singh studied European revolutionary movements and was attracted to anarchist and marxist ideologies. He became involved in numerous revolutionary organisations, quickly rising through the ranks of the Hindustan Republican Association (HRA) to become one of its leaders and was influential in changing its name to Hindustan Socialist Republican Association (HSRA).

Singh was involved in the killing of a British police officer, John Saunders, in revenge for the death of Lala Lajpat Rai at the hands of the police, but the police was unable to capture him. He worked with Batukeshwar Dutt to bomb India's Central Legislative Assembly, and threw leaflets. Held on this charge, he gained support when he underwent a 116 day fast in jail, demanding equal rights for Indian and British political prisoners. During this time, sufficient evidence was brought against him for a conviction in the Saunders case, after trial by a Special Tribunal and appeal at the Privy Council in the UK. He was hanged for his participation in the murder, at the age of 23.

His legacy prompted youths in India to begin fighting for Indian independence and he continues to be a youth idol in modern India as well as the inspiration for a number of films. He is commemorated with a large bronze statue in the Parliament of India, as well as a range of other memorials.

2. The Trial of *Nathuram Godse*

Nathuram Vinayak Godse from the city of Pune, India was a Hindutva activist and journalist, who became notorious as the killer of Mahatma Gandhi. Along with his brother Gopal Godse and six other co-conspirators, he executed a plot to assassinate Gandhi.

Early Life

Nathuram Godse was born in Baramati, Pune District in a Chitpavan Brahmin family. His father, Vinayak Vamanrao Godse, was a post office employee. At birth, he was named Ramachandra.

A commonly held theory suggests that Nathuram was given his name because of an unfortunate incident. Before he was born, his parents had three sons and a daughter, all the three boys died in their infancy. Fearing a curse that targeted male children, young Ramachandra was brought up as a girl for the first few years of his life, including having his nose pierced and being made to wear a nose ring ("Nath" in Marathi). It was then that he earned the nickname "Nathuram" (literally, Ram with a nose ring). After his younger brother was born, they switched to treating him as a boy.

Nathuram Godse attended the local school at Baramati till the fifth standard, after which he was sent to live with an aunt in Pune so that he could study at an English-language school. During his school days, he highly respected Gandhi.

Political Career

Godse dropped out of high school and became an activist with Hindu nationalist organisations such as the Hindu Mahasabha, and the Rashtriya Swayamsevak Sangh (RSS), although the RSS has claimed, he left during the mid-1930s, almost 20 years prior to the assassination. They were particularly opposed to the separatist politics of the All India Muslim League. Godse started a Marathi newspaper for Hindu Mahasabha called *Agrani*, which some years later was renamed as *Hindu Rashtra*. The Hindu Mahasabha had initially backed Gandhi's campaigns of civil disobedience against the British government.

Godse later rejected Gandhi, after what he saw as Gandhi's repeated sabotage against the interests of Hindus by using the blackmailing tactic of "fasting unto death" on many issues. In Godse's view, Gandhi was giving into Muslim interests in ways that seemed unfair and anti-national. He blamed Gandhi for the Partition of India, which left hundreds of thousands of people dead in the wake of religious unrest.

Godse was against Gandhi's personal teachings of extreme or absolutist non-violence. He thought that such non-violent ideology would lead to Hindus losing the will to fight against other religions, which he saw as a matter of self-defence, and thereby becoming permanently enslaved. This has been said to be one of the major reasons behind his decision to kill Gandhi.

Assassination of Mahatma Gandhi

Godse approached Gandhi on January 30, 1948 during the evening prayer and bowed. One of the girls flanking and supporting Gandhi, Abha Chattopadhyay, said to him, "Brother, Bapu is already late," and tried to put him off but he pushed her aside and shot Gandhi in the chest three times at point-blank range with a semi-automatic pistol. Gandhi died almost immediately. After shooting, Godse did not try to run or threaten anyone else. He was attacked and pinned to the ground by the crowd around him and was subsequently arrested when a small group of police officers arrived on the scene a few minutes later.

Trial

Following the assassination of Mahatma Gandhi, he was put on trial beginning May 27, 1948 at Peterhoff, Shimla which housed the Punjab High Court.

On November 8, 1948, Godse delivered his statement in court enunciating the reasons and motives for the assassination.

"As I grew up I developed a tendency to free thinking unfettered by any superstitious allegiance to any isms, political or religious. That is why I worked actively for the eradication of untouchability and the caste system based on birth alone. I openly joined anti-caste movements and maintained that all Hindus are of equal status as to rights, social and religious, and should be considered high or low on merit alone and not through the accident of birth in a particular caste or profession. I used to publicly take part in organised anti-caste dinners which thousands of Hindus, Brahmins, Vaishyas, Kshatriyas, Chamars and Bhangis participated. We broke the caste rules and dined in the company of each other."

— *Nathuram Godse, Answer to the Charge Sheet (Excerpts from Para. 26, 27)*

He listed Dadabhai Naoroji, Swami Vivekananda, Gopal Krishna Gokhale, Bal Gangadhar Tilak as his influences, along with the ancient and modern histories of India, England, France, America and Russia, and the tenets of Socialism and Marxism.

"All this reading and thinking brought me to believe that above all it was my first duty to serve the Hindudom and the Hindu people, as a patriot and even as a humanitarian. For, is it not true that to secure the freedom and to safeguard the just interests of some thirty crores of Hindus constituted the freedom and the well-being of one fifth of human race ? This conviction led me naturally to devote myself to the new Hindu Sanghatanist ideology and programme which alone I came to believe, could win and preserve the national independence of Hindusthan, my Motherland and enable her to render true service to humanity as well."

— *Nathuram Godse, Answer to the Charge Sheet (Para. 28)*

He dismissed Gandhi's policies of truth and non-violence as nothing new or original and considered them implicit in every constitutional public movement. He defended the use of righteous violence against aggression and quoted the examples of Shivaji, Rana Pratap and Guru Govind Singh. He rebuked Gandhi for his "self-conceit" for condemning them as misguided patriots.

He accused Gandhi of paradoxically being a "violent pacifist" who brought calamities to the country through non-violence. According to Godse, Gandhi developed a subjective mentality under which he alone was to be the final judge of what was right or wrong and accused him of having too much power.

"If the country wanted his leadership, it had to accept his infallibility; if it did not, he would stand aloof from the Congress and carry on in his own way. Against such an attitude there can be no halfway house. Either Congress had to surrender its will to his and had to be content with playing second fiddle to all his eccentricity, whimsicality, metaphysics and primitive vision, or it had to carry on without him. He alone was the judge of everyone and everything; he was the master brain guiding the Civil Disobedience Movement; no other could know the technique of that movement. He alone knew when to begin it and when to withdraw it. The movement might succeed or fail, but that could make no difference to the Mahatma's infallibility. 'A Satyagrahi can never fail' was his formula for his own infallibility and nobody except himself knew what a Satyagrahi is."

— *Nathuram Godse, Answer to the Charge Sheet*
(Excerpt from Para. 69)

Godse rebuked Gandhi's "childish insanities and obstinacies". According to Godse, Gandhi did not allow any room for people to disagree with his "irrational" policies. Thus, Godse held Gandhi's irresponsibility as the cause of "blunder after blunder, failure after failure, and disaster after disaster".

Godse accused Gandhi of having a blatant pro-Muslim policy and quoted Gandhi's support for Hindustani (Hindi-Urdu) as the national language of India after the Muslims objected to Hindi and claimed that all of Gandhi's experiments were at the expense of the Hindus.

"Gandhiji began to hold his prayer meetings in a Hindu temple in Bhangi Colony and persisted in reading passages from Quran as a part of the prayer in that Hindu temple in spite of the protest of the Hindu worshippers there. Of course, he dared not read the Gita in a mosque in the teeth of Muslim opposition. He knew what a terrible Muslim reaction would have been if he had done so. But he could safely trample over the feelings of the tolerant Hindu. To belie this belief, I was determined to prove to Gandhiji that the Hindu too could be intolerant when his honour was insulted."

— Nathuram Godse, Answer to the Charge Sheet
(Excerpt from Para. 35)

He explained that Gandhi's unfair treatment and hypocrisy was the cause of his anger.

"The fact that Gandhiji honoured the religious books of Hindus, Muslims and others or that he used to recite during his prayers, verses from the Gita, the Quran and Bible never provoked any ill will in me towards him. To my mind it is not at all objectionable to study comparative religion. Indeed it is a merit."

— Nathuram Godse, Answer to the Charge Sheet
(Excerpt from Para. 48)

He quoted numerous examples of Gandhi's bias such as the fast for the payment of Rs. 55 crores to Pakistan, his support for the Khilafat movement and the invasion of India by the Amir of Afghanistan, his denunciation of the Arya Samaj which included several nationalist leaders, his silence over the subsequent murder of Swami Shraddhanand by a Muslim, his support for the separation of Sind, his placation of Jinnah and the Muslim League, his denial of slaughter and forced conversion of Hindus by Muslims in the Moplah Riots despite evidence to the contrary, opposition to the singing of Vande Mataram, his contrasting treatment of Hindu and Muslim princes, support for cow-slaughter, opposition to Shivaji's Flag, his hypocrisy over the violent Quit India movement (by his call to "Do or Die"), among others. Godse firmly believed in a secular State and was opposed to the supremacist demands of the Muslim League.

Godse accused Gandhi of infatuation with the Muslim League even after the massacre of Hindus by Muslims after Direct Action Day and despite their increasing disloyalty and treason to the Interim Government. He also denounced the Congress, which had boasted of its "nationalism and secularism", of surrendering to Jinnah and accepting Pakistan at the "point of the bayonet".

"This is what Gandhiji had achieved after thirty years of undisputed dictatorship and this is what the Congress Party calls 'Freedom'. Never in the history of the world has such slaughter been officially connived at or the result described as Freedom, and 'Peaceful Transfer of Power'. If what happened in India in 1946, 1947 and 1948 is to be called peaceful, one wonders what would be the violent. Hindu Muslim Unity bubble was finally burst and a theocratic and communal State dissociated from everything that smacked of United India was established with the consent of Nehru and his crowd and they have called it 'Freedom won by them at sacrifice'. Whose sacrifice?"

— Nathuram Godse, Answer to the Charge Sheet
(Excerpt from Para. 69)

According to Godse, Gandhi did not impose any conditions on Muslims because Jinnah and the Muslim League were not at all perturbed or influenced by his fasts and attached no value to his voice. He also criticised Gandhi's epithet "The Father of India" for failing in his paternal duty as he consented to its partition. He claimed Gandhi failed in his duty and proved to be the father of Pakistan.

"His inner-voice, his spiritual power, his doctrine of non-violence of which so much is made of, all crumbled against Jinnah's iron will and proved to be powerless."

— Nathuram Godse, Answer to the Charge Sheet
(Excerpt from Para. 91)

He criticised Gandhi's non-violent policy during the communal clashes: "We should with a cool mind reflect when we are being swept away. Hindus should never be angry against the Muslims even if the latter might make up their minds to undo even their existence. If they put all of us to the sword, we should court death bravely, may they, even rule the world, we shall inhabit the world. At least we should never fear death. We are destined to be born and die; then why need we feel gloomy over it? If all of us die with a smile on our lips, we shall enter a new life. We shall originate a new Hindustan."

"Had this act not been done by me, of course it would have been better for me. But circumstances were beyond my control. So strong was the impulse of my mind that I felt that this man should not be allowed to meet a natural death so that the world may know that he had to pay the penalty of his life for his unjust, anti-national and dangerous favouritism towards a fanatical section of the country. I decided to put an end to this matter and to the further massacre of lacs of Hindus for no fault of theirs. May God now pardon him for his egoistic nature which proved to be too disastrous for the beloved sons of this Holy Land."

— Nathuram Godse, Answer to the Charge Sheet
(Excerpt from Para. 140)

Godse foresaw that he would be hated by the people, his future would be totally ruined, and that he would lose all his honour, which he held more valuable than his life, if he were to assassinate Gandhi. However, he considered that Indian politics in Gandhi's absence would be practical, able to retaliate and be powerful with the armed forces, and that "the nation would be saved from the inroads of Pakistan".

He then confessed that he fired the shots at Gandhi on January 30, 1948, on the prayer-grounds in Birla House.

"I do say that my shots were fired at the person whose policy and action had brought rack and ruin and destruction to millions of Hindus. There was no legal machinery by which such an offender could be brought to book and for this reason I fired those fatal shots. I bear no ill will towards anyone individually, but I do say that I had no respect for the present government owing to their policy, which was unfairly favourable towards the Muslims. But at the same time I could clearly see that the policy was entirely due to the presence of Gandhi."

— Nathuram Godse, Answer to the Charge Sheet
(Excerpt from Para. 135)

He then accused Prime Minister Nehru of hypocrisy with his speeches of secularism, because he was instrumental in creating the Islamic state of Pakistan along with Gandhi's persistent policy of appeasement towards the Muslims.

"Finally, I now stand before the court to accept the full share of my responsibility for what I have done and the judge would, of course, pass against me such orders of sentence as may be considered proper. But I would like to add that I do not desire any mercy to be shown to me, nor do I wish that anyone should beg for mercy on my behalf. My confidence about the moral side of my action has not been shaken even by the criticism levelled against it on all sides. I have no doubt that honest writers of history will weigh my act and find the true value thereof someday in future."

— Nathuram Godse, Answer to the Charge Sheet
(Excerpt from Para. 150)

In the light of the statement, Justice Khosla commented :

"The highlight of the appeal before us was the discourse delivered by Nathuram Godse in his defence. He spoke for several hours, discussing, in the first instance, the facts of the case and then the motive, which had prompted him to take Mahatma Gandhi's life.

The audience was visibly and audibly moved. There was a deep silence when he ceased speaking. Many women were in tears and men coughing and searching for their handkerchiefs. The silence was accentuated and made deeper by the sound of an occasional subdued sniff or a muffled cough.

I have, however, no doubt that had the audience of that day been constituted into a jury and entrusted with the task of deciding Godse's appeal, they would have brought in a verdict of 'not guilty' by an over-whelming majority."

Execution

On November 8, 1949, Godse was sentenced to death. Among those calling for commutation of the death sentence for the defendants were Jawaharlal Nehru, as well as Gandhi's two sons, who felt that executing their father's killers would dishonour his memory and legacy which included a staunch opposition to the death penalty. Godse was hanged at Ambala Jail on November 15, 1949, along with Narayan Apte, the other conspirator. Savarkar was also charged with conspiracy in the assassination of Gandhi, but was acquitted and subsequently released.

Aftermath

Millions of Indians mourned Gandhi's assassination. The Hindu Mahasabha was vilified and the Rashtriya Swayamsevak Sangh, the RSS, was temporarily banned. However, investigators could find no evidence that the RSS bureaucracy had formally sponsored or even knew of Godse's plot. The RSS ban was lifted by Prime Minister Nehru and Sardar Vallabhbhai Patel in 1949. The RSS, to this day denies any connection with Godse, and disputes the claim that he was a member.

After the assassination, many criticised the Indian government for not doing more to protect Gandhi who, earlier in the week, had been the target of a bomb plot by the same conspirators who later shot him. Of particular concern, was the fact that a Bombay detective had wired the names and descriptions of the assassins along with the fact that they were known to be in Delhi stalking Gandhi. On the other hand, Gandhi had repeatedly refused to cooperate with his own security and had resigned himself to a violent death which he accepted as an inevitable part of his destiny.

Nathuram Godse

Born : May 19, 1910

Died: November 15, 1949

A Hindutva activist who assassinated Mahatma Gandhi.

Born in a devotional Brahmin family, he instinctively came to revere Hindu religion, Hindu history and Hindu culture. During his trial, he mentioned that he had no personal hatred of Gandhi.

3. The Trial of *Vinayak Damodar Savarkar*

Vinayak Damodar Savarkar was an Indian freedom fighter, revolutionary and politician. Savarkar was also a poet, writer and playwright.

Savarkar's revolutionary activities began when studying in India and England, where he was associated with the India House and founded student societies including Abhinav Bharat Society and the Free India Society, as well as publications espousing the cause of complete Indian independence by revolutionary means. Savarkar published *The Indian War of Independence* about the Indian rebellion of 1857 that was banned by British authorities. He was arrested in 1910 for his connections with the revolutionary group India House. Following a failed attempt to escape while being transported from Marseilles, Savarkar was sentenced to two life terms amounting to 50 years' imprisonment and moved to the Cellular Jail in the Andaman and Nicobar Islands.

While in jail, Savarkar wrote the work describing *Hindutva*, openly espousing Hindu nationalism. He was released in 1921 under restrictions after signing a plea for clemency in which he renounced revolutionary activities. Travelling widely, Savarkar became a forceful orator and writer, advocating Hindu political and social unity. Serving as the president of the Hindu Mahasabha, Savarkar endorsed the ideal of India as a *Hindu Rashtra* and opposed the Quit India struggle in 1942, calling it a "Quit India but keep your army" movement. He became a fierce critic of the Indian National Congress and its acceptance of India's partition, and was one of those accused in the assassination of Indian leader Mohandas Karamchand Gandhi. He was acquitted as the charges could not be proven.

Early Life

Vinayak was born in the family of Damodar and Radhabai Savarkar in the village of Bhagur, near the city of Nasik, Maharashtra. He had three other siblings namely Ganesh, Narayan, and a sister named Mainabai.

After death of parents, the eldest sibling Ganesh known as Babarao, took responsibility of the family. Babarao played a supportive and influential role in Vinayak's teenage life. During this period, Vinayak organised a youth group called *Mitra Mela* (Band of Friends) and encouraged revolutionary and nationalist views of passion using this group. In 1901, Vinayak Savarkar married Yamunabai, daughter of Ramchandra Triambak Chiplunkar, who supported his university education. Subsequently in 1902, he enrolled in Fergusson College, Pune (then Poona). As a young man, he was inspired by the new generation of radical political leaders namely Bal Gangadhar Tilak, Bipin Chandra Pal and Lala Lajpat Rai along with the political struggle against the partition of Bengal and the rising Swadeshi campaign. He was involved in various nationalist activities at various levels. In 1905, during Dussehra festivities Vinayak organised setting up of a bonfire of foreign goods and clothes. Along with his fellow students and friends he formed a political outfit called *Abhinav Bharat*. Vinayak was soon expelled from college due to his activities but was still permitted to take his Bachelor of Arts degree examinations. After completing his degree, nationalist activist Shyam Krishnavarma helped Vinayak to go to England to study law, on a scholarship. It was during this period that *Garam Dal*, (literally translated as Hot Faction) was formed under the leadership of Tilak, due to the split of Indian National Congress. The members of *Garam Dal*, did not acknowledge the moderate Indian National Congress leadership agenda which advocated dialogue and reconciliation with the British Raj. Tilak advocated the philosophy of Swaraj and was soon imprisoned for his support of revolutionary activities.

Activities at India House

After his joining Gray's Inn law college in London, Vinayak took accommodation at India House. Organised by expatriate social and political activist Pandit Shyamji, India House was a thriving centre for student political activities. Savarkar soon founded the

Free India Society to help organise fellow Indian students with the goal of fighting for complete independence through a revolution, declaring –

"We must stop complaining about this British officer or that officer, this law or that law. There would be no end to that. Our movement must not be limited to being against any particular law, but it must be for acquiring the authority to make laws itself. In other words, we want absolute independence."

Savarkar envisioned a guerrilla war for independence along the lines of the famous armed uprising of 1857. Studying the history of the revolt, from English as well as Indian sources, Savarkar wrote the book, *The History of the War of Indian Independence*. He analysed the circumstances of 1857 uprising and assailed British rule in India as unjust and oppressive. It was via this book that Savarkar became one of the first writers to allude the uprising as India's first war for independence. The book was banned from publication throughout the British Empire. Madame Bhikaji Cama, and expatriate Indian revolutionary obtained its publication in the Netherlands, France and Germany. Widely smuggled and circulated, the book attained great popularity and influenced rising young Indians. Savarkar was studying revolutionary methods and he came into contact with a veteran of the Russian Revolution of 1905, who imparted him the knowledge of bomb-making. Savarkar had printed and circulated a manual amongst his friends, on bomb-making and other methods of guerrilla warfare. In 1909, Madan Lal Dhingra, a keen follower and friend of Savarkar, assassinated British MP Sir Curzon Wylie in a public meeting. Dhingra's action provoked controversy across Britain and India, evoking enthusiastic admiration as well as condemnation. Savarkar published an article in which he all but endorsed the murder and worked to organise support, both political and for Dhingra's legal defence. At a meeting of Indians called for a condemnation of Dhingra's deed, Savarkar protested the intention of condemnation and was drawn into a hot debate and angry scuffle with other attendants. A secretive and restricted trial and a sentence awarding the death penalty to Dhingra provoked an outcry and protest across the Indian students and political community. Strongly protesting the verdict, Savarkar struggled with British authorities in laying claim to

Dhingra's remains following his execution. Savarkar hailed Dhingra as a hero and martyr, and began encouraging revolution with greater intensity.

Arrest in London and in Marseilles

In India, Ganesh Savarkar had organised an armed revolt against the Morley-Minto reforms of 1909. The British police implicated Savarkar in the investigation for allegedly plotting the crime. Hoping to evade arrest, Savarkar moved to Madame Cama's home in Paris. He was nevertheless arrested by police on March 13, 1910. In the final days of freedom, Savarkar wrote letters to a close friend planning his escape. Knowing that he would most likely be shipped to India, Savarkar asked his friend to keep track of which ship and route he would be taken through. When the ship *S.S. Morea* reached the port of Marseilles on July 8, 1910, Savarkar escaped from his cell through a porthole and dived into the water, swimming to the shore in the hope that his friend would be there to receive him in a car. But his friend was late in arriving, and the alarm having been raised, Savarkar was re arrested.

Savarkar Case

Savarkar's arrest at Marseilles caused the French government to protest to the British. This dispute came before the Permanent Court of International Arbitration in 1910, and it gave its decision in 1911. The case excited much controversy as was reported by the New York Times, and it considered that it involved an interesting international question of the right of asylum. The Court held, firstly, that since there was a pattern of collaboration between the two countries regarding the possibility of Savarkar's escape in Marseilles and since there was neither force nor fraud in inducing the French authorities to return Savarkar to them, the British authorities did not have to hand him back to the French in order for the latter to hold rendition proceedings. On the other hand, the tribunal also observed that there had been an irregularity in Savarkar's arrest and delivery over to the Indian Army Military Police guard.

Trial

Arriving in Mumbai (colonial name Bombay), he was taken to the Yeravda Central Jail. Following a trial, Savarkar was sentenced to 50 years imprisonment and transported on July 4, 1911 to the infamous Cellular Jail in the Andaman and Nicobar Islands.

His fellow captives included many political prisoners, who were forced to perform hard labour for many years. Reunited with his brother Ganesh, the Savarkars nevertheless struggled in the harsh environment. Forced to rise at 5 a.m., tasks including cutting trees and chopping wood, and working at the oil mill under regimental strictness, with talking amidst prisoners strictly prohibited during mealtime. Prisoners were subject to frequent mistreatment and torture. Contact with the outside world and home was restricted to writing and mailing of one letter a year. In these years, Savarkar withdrew within himself and performed his routine tasks mechanically. Obtaining permission to start a rudimentary jail library, Savarkar would also teach some fellow convicts to read and write.

Savarkar appealed for clemency in 1911 and again during Sir Reginald Craddock's visit in 1913, citing poor health in the oppressive conditions. In 1920, the Indian National Congress and leaders such as Mahatma Gandhi, Vithalbhai Patel and Bal Gangadhar Tilak demanded his unconditional release. Savarkar tactically signed a statement endorsing the trial, verdict and British law, and renouncing violence, a bargain for freedom.

"I hereby acknowledge that I had a fair trial and just sentence. I heartily abhor methods of violence resorted to in days gone by and I feel myself duty bound to uphold law and constitution to the best of my powers and I am willing to make the 1919 Montague-Chelmsford Reforms a success in so far as I may be allowed to do so in future."

Savarkar appealed for clemency within a year of his reaching the Andamans. In one of his communications, he says,

"If the government in their manifold beneficence and mercy release me, I for one cannot but be the staunchest advocate of constitutional progress and loyalty to the English government which is the foremost condition of that progress.... Moreover, my conversion to the constitutional line would bring back all those misled young men in India and abroad who were once looking up to me as their guide."

On May 2, 1921, the Savarkar brothers were moved to a jail in Ratnagiri, and later to the Yeravda Central Jail. He was finally released on January 6, 1924 under stringent restrictions – he was not to leave

Ratnagiri District and was to refrain from political activities for the next five years. However, police restrictions on his activities would not be dropped until provincial autonomy was granted in 1937. Puniyani considered Savarkar to be a coward for submitting such clemency offers, and noted that Savarkar's anti-British struggles and anti-British activities totally ceased after his release by the British as per the terms of his internment. Joglekar calls such allegations a Marxist Calumny and considers Savarkar's appeal for clemency a tactical ploy, like Shivaji's letter to Aurangzeb, during his arrest at Agra, Vladimir Lenin's travel by sealed train through Germany as a part of a deal with Germany and Joseph Stalin's pact with Adolf Hitler. Joglekar noted that Shivaji made many promises to Aurangzeb which he did not keep after his escape which was the same done by Savarkar comprimising his patriotism.

Hindutva

During his incarceration, Savarkar's views began turning increasingly towards Hindu cultural and political nationalism, and the next phase of his life remained dedicated to this cause. In the brief period he spent at the Ratnagiri jail, Savarkar wrote his ideological treatise – *Hindutva: Who is a Hindu?* Smuggled out of the prison, it was published by Savarkar's supporters under his alias "Maharatta". In this work, Savarkar promoted a radical new vision of Hindu social and political consciousness. Savarkar began describing a "Hindu" as a patriotic inhabitant of Bharatavarsha, venturing beyond a religious identity. While emphasising the need for patriotic and social unity of all Hindu communities, he described Hinduism, Jainism, Sikhism and Buddhism as one and same. He outlined his vision of a "Hindu Rashtra" (Hindu Nation) as "Akhand Bharat" (United India), purportedly stretching across the entire Indian subcontinent.

Scholars, historians and Indian politicians have been divided in their interpretation of Savarkar's ideas. A self-described atheist, Savarkar regards being Hindu as a cultural and political identity. While often stressing social and community unity between Hindus, Sikhs, Buddhists and Jains, Savarkar's notions of loyalty to the fatherland are seen as an implicit criticism of Muslims and Christians who regard Mecca, Medina and Jerusalem as their holiest places. Savarkar openly assailed what he saw as Muslim political separatism, arguing that the loyalty of many Muslims was conflicted. After his release, Savarkar founded the Ratnagiri Hindu Sabha on January 23, 1924, aiming to work for the social and cultural preservation of Hindu heritage and civilisation. Becoming a frequent and forceful orator, Sarvakar agitated for the use of Hindi as a common national language and against caste discrimination and untouchability. Focusing his energies on writing, Savarkar authored the *Hindu Pad-pada-shahi* – a book documenting and extolling the Maratha empire and *My Transportation for Life* – an account of his early revolutionary days, arrest, trial and incarceration. He also wrote and published a collection of poems, plays and novels. Another activity he started was to reconvert to Hinduism those who had converted to other faiths.

Leader of the Hindu Mahasabha

Although disavowing revolution and politics, Savarkar grew disenchanted with the Congress's emphasis of non-violence and criticised Gandhi for suspending Non-cooperation Movement following the killing of 22 policemen in Chauri Chaura in 1922. He soon joined the Hindu Mahasabha, a political party founded in 1911 and avowed to Hindu political rights and empowerment. The party was disengaged from the Indian independence movement, allowing Savarkar to work without British interference. As his travel restrictions weakened, Savarkar began travelling extensively, delivering speeches, exhorting Hindu political unity and criticising the Congress and Muslim politicians. Savarkar and the Mahasabha did not endorse the Salt Satyagraha launched by the Congress in 1930, and neither Savarkar nor any of his supporters participated in Civil Disobedience. Savarkar focused on expanding the party's membership, revamping its structure and delivering its message.

In the wake of the rising popularity of the Muslim League led by Muhammad Ali Jinnah, Savarkar and his party began gaining traction in the national political environment. Savarkar moved to Mumbai and was elected president of the Hindu Mahasabha in 1937, and would serve until 1943. The Congress swept the polls in 1937 but conflicts between the Congress and Jinnah would exacerbate Hindu-Muslim political divisions. Jinnah derided Congress rule as a "Hindu Raj", and hailed December 22, 1939 as a "Day of Deliverance" for Muslims when the Congress resigned en masse in protest of India's arbitrary inclusion into World War II. Savarkar's message of Hindu unity and empowerment gained increasing popularity amidst the worsening communal climate. However, Savarkar and the Mahasabha joined several political parties including the League and the Communist Party of India in endorsing the war effort. Savarkar publicly encouraged Hindus to enlist in the military, which his supporters described as an effort for Hindus to obtain military training and experience potentially useful in a future confrontation with the British. When the Congress launched the Quit India rebellion in 1942, Savarkar criticised the rebellion and asked Hindus to stay active in the war effort and not disobey the government. Under his leadership, the Mahasabha won several seats in the central and provincial legislatures. Hindu Mahasabha activists protested Gandhi's initiative to hold talks with Jinnah in 1944, which Savarkar denounced as "appeasement". He assailed the British proposals for transfer of power, attacking both the Congress and the British for making concessions to Muslim separatists. Soon after Independence, Dr Shyama Prasad Mookerjee resigned as Vice-President of the Hindu Mahasabha dissociating himself from its Akhand Hindustan plank, which implied undoing partition.

Opposition to the Partition of India

The Muslim League adopted the Lahore Resolution in 1940, calling for a separate Muslim state based on the *Two-Nation Theory*, Bhimrao Ramji Ambedkar summaries Savarkar's position, in his *Pakistan or The Partition of India* as follows,

"Mr. Savarkar... insists that, although there are two nations in India, India shall not be divided into two parts, one for Muslims and the other for the Hindus; that the two nations shall dwell in one country and shall live under the mantle of one single constitution. In the struggle for political power between the two nations the rule of the game which Mr. Savarkar prescribes is to be one man one vote, be the man Hindu or Muslim. In his scheme a Muslim is to have no advantage which a Hindu does not have. Minority is to be no justification for privilege and majority is to be no ground for penalty. The State will guarantee the Muslims any defined measure of political power in the form of Muslim religion and Muslim culture. But the State will not guarantee secured seats in the Legislature or in the Administration and, if such guarantee is insisted upon by the Muslims, such guaranteed quota is not to exceed their proportion to the general population."

Arrest and Acquittal in Gandhi's Assassination

Following the assassination of Gandhi on January 30, 1948, police arrested the assassin Pundit Nathuram Godse and his alleged accomplices and conspirators. He was a member of the Hindu Mahasabha and RSS's Swayansevak, an organisation started by among others Pundit Madan Mohan Malviya and Lala Lajpat Rai. Godse was the editor of Agrani – Hindu Rashtra a Marathi daily from Pune which was run by a company "The Hindu Rashtra Prakashan Ltd." This company had contributions from such eminent persons as Gulabchand Hirachand, Bhalji Pendharkar and Jugalkishore Birla. Savarkar had invested 15,000 in the company. Savarkar a former president of the Hindu Mahasabha, was arrested on 5 February 1948, from his house in Shivaji Park, and kept under detention in the Arthur Road Prison, Mumbai. He was charged with murder, conspiracy to murder and abetment to murder. Ambedkar secretly assured Savarkar's lawyer, Mr. L.B. Bhopatkar that his client was implicated as a murder-suspect on the flimsiest grounds.

The Approver's Testimony

Godse claimed full responsibility for planning and carrying out the attack. According to Badge, the approver, on 17 January, 1948, Nathuram Godse went to have a last *darshan* of Savarkar in Bombay before the assassination. While Badge and Shankar waited outside, Nathuram and Apte went in. On coming out Apte told Badge that Savarkar blessed them "*Yashasvi houn ya*" (be successful and return). Apte also said that Savarkar predicted that Gandhiji's 100 years were over and there was no doubt that the task would be successfully finished. However, Badge's testimony was not accepted as the approver's evidence lacked independent corroboration and hence Savarkar was acquitted.

Kapur Commission

On November 12, 1964, a religious programme was organised in Pune to celebrate the release of the Gopal Godse, Madanlal Pahwa, Vishnu Karkare from jail after the expiry of their sentences. Dr. G. V. Ketkar, grandson of Bal Gangadhar Tilak, former editor of *Kesari* and then editor of *Tarun Bharat*, who presided over the function, revealed the information of a conspiracy to kill Gandhi, about which he professed knowledge, six months before the act. Ketkar was arrested. A public furore ensued both outside and inside the Maharashtra Legislative Assembly and both houses of the Indian Parliament. Under pressure of 29 members of Parliament and public opinion, the then Union home minister Gulzarilal Nanda appointed Gopal Swarup Pathak, M. P. and a senior advocate of the Supreme Court of India, in charge of inquiry of conspiracy to murder Gandhi. The central government intended on conducting a thorough inquiry with the help of old records in consultation with the government of Maharashtra, Pathak was given three months to conduct his inquiry, subsequently Jevanlal Kapur a retired judge of the Supreme Court of India was appointed to conduct the inquiry. The Kapur Commission was provided with evidence not produced in the court; especially the testimony of two of Savarkar's close aides – Appa Ramachandra Kasar, his bodyguard, and Gajanan Vishnu Damle, his secretary. Kasar told the Kapur Commission that Godse and Apte visited Savarkar on or about January 23 or 24, which was when they returned from Delhi after the bomb incident. Damle deposed that Godse and Apte saw Savarkar in the middle of January and sat with him (Savarkar) in his garden. Justice Kapur concluded: "All these facts taken together were destructive of any theory other than the conspiracy to murder by Savarkar and his group."

Later Life and Death

Despite his exoneration, Savarkar's role in the plot remains a source of intense controversy but at the time the public held him answerable for instigating the murder. Public outrage over Gandhi's murder wrecked the fortunes of the Hindu Mahasabha, whose membership and activity dwindled into insignificance. Savarkar's home in Mumbai was stoned by angry mobs, and his political influence and activism sharply curtailed by widespread public anger. His activities remained confined to occasional speeches and publishing his writings.

He considered RSS and its associate organisations with equal ideology. But RSS had a stronger appeal to the votaries of Hindutva. RSS founder Keshav Baliram Hedgewar had the highest respect for Savarkar, and RSS continues to acknowledge Savarkar's efforts for the Hindu unity. Savarkar also admired and participated in the activities of RSS.

In 1966 Savarkar renounced medicines, food and water leading to his death on February 26, 1966. He was mourned by large crowds that attended his cremation. He had written an article – Atma-hatya or Deh-tyaag, arguing that suicide in most cases is taking one's life, but renouncing life after the body was no longer capable of functioning properly was a different matter. He left behind a son Vishwas and a daughter Prabha Chiplunkar. His first son, Prabhakar, had died in infancy. His home, possessions and other personal relics have been preserved for public display.

Savarkar was a national and political 'non-entity' in independent India by the time he died and thereafter. After his death, since Savarkar was championing militarisation, some thought that it would be fitting if his mortal remains were to be carried on a gun-carriage. A request to that effect was made to the then Defence Minister, Y.B. Chavan, who later on became Deputy Prime Minister of India. But Chavan turned down the proposal and not a single minister from the Maharashtra Cabinet showed up in the cremation ground to pay homage to Savarkar. In New Delhi, the Speaker of the Parliament turned down a request that it pay homage to Savarkar. In fact, after the independence of India, Jawaharlal Nehru had put forward a proposal to demolish the Cellular Jail in the Andamans and build a hospital in its place. When Y.B. Chavan, as the Home Minister of India, went to the Andamans, he was asked whether he would like to visit Savarkar's jail but he was not interested. Also when Morarji Desai went as Prime Minister to the Andamans, he too refused to visit Savarkar's cell. Savarkar's contribution to Indian Freedom Struggle has been immense, starting from his student days in London, where he organised the Indians in England, and France from the famous India House, wrote the famous book *First Indian War of Independence,* inspiring Indians to remember martyrs of 1857, and motivating them to carry on second war of independence. English government at that time, arrested him on political charges of waging a war against the English king, for which he was sentenced to 50 years of imprisonment, in 1907 which was unheard of in Indian political circles. No Congress politician was sentenced to such a long and rigorous imprisonment. His entire life was devoted to bring India freedom, from his works and actions.

Vinayak Damodar Savarkar

Born: May 28, 1883

Died: February 26, 1966

A freedom fighter, social reformer, writer, political leader and philosopher.

Vinayak Damodar Savarkar launched a movement for religious reform advocating dismantling the system of caste in Hindu culture, and reconversion of the converted Hindus back to Hindu religion. Savarkar created the term *Hindutva*, and emphasised its distinctiveness from Hinduism which he associated with social and political disunity. Savarkar's *Hindutva* sought to create an inclusive collective identity. The five elements of Savarkar's philosophy were Utilitarianism, Rationalism and Positivism, Humanism and Universalism, Pragmatism and Realism.

The airport at Port Blair, Andaman and Nicobar's capital, has been named Veer Savarkar International Airport. The commemorative blue plaque on India House fixed by the Historic Building and Monuments Commission for England reads: "Vinayak Damodar Savarkar, 1883-1966, Indian patriot and philosopher lived here".

4. The INA Trials

The INA trials or the Red Fort Trials refer to the courts martial of a number of officers of the Indian National Army between November 1945 and May 1946 variously for treason, torture, murder and abetment to murder. The first, and most famous, of the approximately ten trials was held in the Red Fort in Delhi, hence deriving the name. In total, approximately ten courts-martial were held. The first of these, and the most celebrated one, was the joint court-martial of Colonel Prem Sahgal, Colonel Gurubaksh Singh Dhillon and Major General Shah Nawaz Khan. The three had been officers in the British Indian Army and taken prisoners of war in Malaya or Singapore. They had, like a large number of other troops and officers of the British Indian Army, joined the Indian National Army and later fought in Imphal and Burma alongside the Japanese forces in allegiance to Azad Hind. These three came to be the only defendants in the INA trials who were charged of "Waging War against the King Emperor" (The Indian Army act of 1911 did not have a separate charge for treason) as well as murder and abetment of murder. Those charged later only faced trial for torture and murder or abetment of murder. The trials covered arguments based on Military Law, Constitutional Law, International Law, and Politics. These trials attracted much publicity, and public sympathy for the defendants who were perceived as patriots in India, and outcry over the grounds of the trial, as well as general emerging unease and unrest within the troops of the Raj ultimately forced the then Army Chief Claude Auchinleck to commute the sentences of the three defendants in the first trial.

Indian National Army

Japan, as well as South East Asia was a major refuge for Indian nationalists living in exile before the start of World War II who formed strong proponents of militant nationalism and also influenced Japanese policy significantly. Although Japanese intentions and policies with regards to India were far from concrete at the start of the war, Japan had sent intelligence missions, notably under Major I Fujiwara, into South Asia even before the start of the World War II to garner support from the Malayan Sultans, the Burmese resistance and the Indian movement. These missions were successful establishing contacts with Indian nationalists in exile in Thailand and Malaya, supporting the establishment and organisation of the Indian Independence League.

At the outbreak of World War II in South East Asia, 70,000 Indian troops were stationed in Malaya. After the start of the war, Japan's spectacular Malayan Campaign had brought under her control considerable of Indian prisoners of war, notably nearly 55,000 after the fall of Singapore. The conditions of service within the British Indian Army as well as the conditions in Malaya had fed dissension among these troops. From these troops, the First Indian National Army was formed under Mohan Singh Deb and received considerable Japanese aid and support. It was formally proclaimed in September 1942 and declared the subordinate military wing of the Indian Independence League in June that year. The unit was dissolved in December 1942 after apprehensions of Japanese motives with regards to the INA led to disagreements and distrust between Mohan Singh and INA leadership on one hand, and the leagues leadership, most notable Rash Behari Bose. The arrival of Subhas Bose in June 1943 saw the revival and reorganisation of the unit as the army of The Azad Hind govt. that was formed in October 1943. Within days of its proclamation in October 1943, the Government had been accorded recognition by Germany, Fascist Italy, Croatia, Thailand, Ba Maw's Burmese government, and some other Axis-allied nations, as well as receiving felicitations and gifts from the government of neutral Ireland and Irish republicans. The Azad Hind government declared war on Britain and America in October 1943. In Nov 1943, Azad Hind had been given a limited form of governmental jurisdiction over the Andaman and Nicobar Islands, which had been captured by the

Imperial Japanese Navy early in the war. In the early part of 1944, INA forces were in action along with the Japanese forces in Imphal and Kohima area against commonwealth forces, and later fell back with the retreating Japanese forces after the failed campaign. In early 1945, the INA's troops were committed against the successful Allied Burma Campaign. A vast number of INA troops were captured, defected or fell otherwise into British hands during the Burma campaign by end of March that year and by the time Rangoon fell in May 1945, the INA had more or less ceased to exist although some activities continued till Singapore was recaptured.

At the conclusion of the World War II, the government of British India brought some of the captured INA soldiers to trial on treason charges. The prisoners would potentially face the death penalty, life imprisonment or a fine as punishment if found guilty.

Early Trials

By 1943 and 1944, courts martial were taking place in India of former personnel of the British Indian Army who were captured fighting in INA ranks or working in support of the INA's subversive activities. These did not receive any publicity or political sympathies and support till much later. These charges in these earlier trials were of "Committing a civil offence contrary to the Section 41 of the Indian Army Act, 1911 or the Section 41 of the Burma Army Act" with the offence specified as "Waging War against the King" contrary to the Section 121 of the Indian Penal Code and the Burma Penal Code as relevant.

Red Fort Trial

However, the number of INA troops captured by Commonwealth forces by the end of the Burma Campaign made it necessary to take a selective policy to charge those accused of the worst allegations. The first of these was the joint trial of Shah Nawaz Khan, Prem Sahgal and Gurubaksh Singh Dhillon, followed by the trials of Abdul Rashid, Shinghara Singh, and Fateh Khan. The decision was made to hold a public trial, as opposed to the earlier trials, and given the political importance and significance of the trials, the decision was made to hold these at the Red Fort. Also, due to the complexity of the case, the provision was made under the Indian Army Act rule 82(a) for counsels to appear for defence and prosecution. The then Advocate

General of India, Sir Naushirwan P Engineer was appointed the counsel for prosecution. The accused were offered the help of both the INA Defence Committee formed by the Indian National Congress and, for the Muslims amongst the accused, the Defence committee formed by the Muslim League.

INA Defence Committee

The Indian National Congress and the Muslim League both made the release of the three defendants an important political issue during the agitation for independence of 1945-46.

First Trial

The first trial was held between November and December 1945. The charges against the three accused were:

Against Gurubaksh Singh Dhillon

- Waging War against the King contrary to the section 121 of the Indian Penal Code.
- Four charges of murder contrary to the Section 302 of the Indian Penal code.

Against Prem Sahgal

- Waging War against the King contrary to the section 121 of the Indian Penal Code.
- Four charges of abetment of murder in the charges brought against Gurubaksh Singh Dhillon contrary to Section 109 of the Indian Penal Code.

Against Shah Nawaz

- Waging War against the King contrary to the section 121 of the Indian Penal Code.
- One charge of abetment of murder in the charges brought against Gurubaksh Singh Dhillon contrary to Section 109 of the Indian Penal Code.

The charge of Waging War consisted of planning, organisation and participation in military operations between September 1942 and April 1945.

The murder and abetment charges concerned the shooting of INA members for desertion and attempting to communicate with the enemy in the Popa Hill area of Burma contrary to Section 35 of the INA act.

Second Trial

These were the trials of Abdul Rashid, Shinghara Singh, and Fateh Khan. In light of unrest over the charges of treason and glorification in the first trial, the charges of treason was dropped. The site of trial was also moved from the Red Fort to an adjoining building.

Consequences of the Trials

Beyond the concurrent campaigns of non-cooperation and non-violent protest, this spread to include mutinies and wavering support within the British Indian Army. This movement marked the last major campaign in which the forces of the Congress and the Muslim League aligned together; the Congress tricolour and the green flag of the League were flown together at protests. In spite of this aggressive and widespread opposition, the court martial was carried out, and all three defendants were sentenced to deportation for life. This sentence, however, was never carried out, as the immense public pressure of the demonstrations forced Claude Auchinleck, Commander-in-Chief of the Indian Army to release all three defendants.

During the trial, mutiny broke out in the Royal Indian Navy, incorporating ships and shore establishments of the RIN throughout India, from Karachi to Bombay and from Vizag to Calcutta. The most significant, if disconcerting factor for the Raj, was the significant militant public support that it received. At some places, NCOs in the British Indian Army started ignoring orders from British superiors. In Madras and Pune, the British garrisons had to face revolts within the ranks of the British Indian Army.

Another Army mutiny took place at Jabalpur during the last week of February 1946, soon after the Navy mutiny at Bombay. This was suppressed by force, including the use of the bayonet by British troops. It lasted about two weeks. After the mutiny, about 45 persons were tried by court martial. 41 were sentenced to varying terms of imprisonment or dismissal. In addition, a large number were discharged on administrative grounds. While the participants of the Naval mutiny were given the freedom fighters' pension, the Jabalpur mutineers got nothing. They even lost their service pension.

Reflecting on the factors that guided the British decision to relinquish the Raj in India, Clement Attlee, the then British Prime Minister, cited several reasons, the most important of which were the INA activities of Netaji Subhas Chandra Bose, which weakened the Indian Army – the foundation of the British Empire in India and the RIN mutiny that made the British realise that the Indian armed forces could no longer be trusted to prop up the Raj. Although Britain had made, at the time of the Cripps' mission in 1942, a commitment to grant dominion status to India after the war this suggests that, contrary to the usual narrative of India's independence struggle, (which generally focuses on Congress and Mahatma Gandhi), the INA and the revolts, mutinies, and public resentment it germinated were an important factor in the complete withdrawal of the Raj from India.

Most of the INA. soldiers were set free after cashiering and forfeiture of pay and allowance. On the recommendation of Lord Mountbatten of Burma, and agreed by Nehru, as a precondition for Independence, the INA soldiers were not reinducted into the Indian Army.

Whether as a measure of the pain that the allies suffered in Imphal and Burma or as an act of vengeance, Mountbatten, Head of Southeast Asia Command, ordered the INA Memorial to its fallen soldiers destroyed when Singapore was recaptured in 1945. It has been suggested later that Mountbatten's actions may have been to erase completely the records of INA's existence, to prevent the seeds of the idea of a revolutionary socialist liberation force from spreading into the vestiges of its colonies amidst the spectre of cold-war politics already taking shape at the time, and had haunted the Colonial powers before the war. In 1995, the National Heritage Board of Singapore marked the place as a historical site. A Cenotaph has since been erected at the site where the memorial stood.

After the war ended, the story of the INA and the Free India Legion was seen as so inflammatory that, fearing mass revolts and uprisings – not just in India, but across its empire – the British Government forbad the BBC from broadcasting their story. However, the stories of the trials at the Red Fort filtered through. Newspapers reported at the time of the trials that some of the INA soldiers held at Red Fort had been executed, which only succeeded in causing further protests.

INA

The Indian National Army (INA) or Azad Hind Fauj was an armed force formed by Indian nationalists in 1942 in Southeast Asia during World War II. The aim of the army was to overthrow the British Raj in colonial India, with Japanese assistance. Initially composed of Indian prisoners of war captured by Japan in the Malayan campaign and at Singapore, it later drew volunteers from Indian expatriate population in Malaya and Burma.

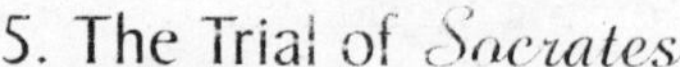

5. The Trial of *Socrates*

The trial and execution of Socrates in Athens in 399 B.C.E. puzzles historians. Why, in a society enjoying more freedom and democracy than any the world had ever seen, would a seventy-year-old philosopher be put to death for what he was teaching? The puzzle is all the greater because Socrates had taught – without molestation – all of his adult life. What could Socrates have said or done than prompted a jury of 500 Athenians to send him to his death just a few years before he would have died naturally?

Finding an answer to the mystery of the trial of Socrates is complicated by the fact that the two surviving accounts of the defense (or apology) of Socrates both come from disciples of his, Plato and Xenophon. Historians suspect that Plato and Xenophon, intent on showing their master in a favourable light, failed to present in their accounts the most damning evidence against Socrates.

What appears almost certain is that the decisions to prosecute and ultimately convict Socrates had a lot to do with the turbulent history of Athens in the several years preceding his trial. An examination of that history may not provide final answers, but it does provide important clues.

Background

Socrates, the son of a sculptor (or stonecutter) and a midwife, was a young boy when the rise to power of Pericles brought on the dawning of the "Golden Age of Greece." As a young man, Socrates saw a fundamental power shift, as Pericles – perhaps history's first liberal politician – acted on his belief that the masses, and not just property-owning aristocrats, deserved liberty. Pericles created the people's courts and used the public treasury to promote the arts. He pushed ahead with an unprecedented building program designed not only to demonstrate the glory that was Greece, but also to ensure full

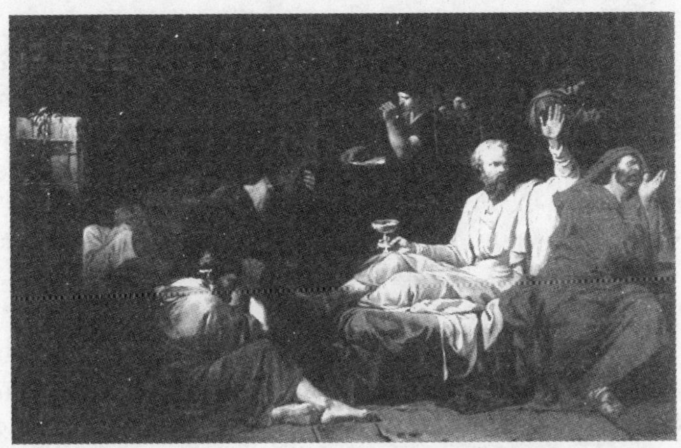

employment and provide opportunities for wealth creation among the unpropertied class. The rebuilding of the Acropolis and the construction of the Parthenon were the two best known of Pericles' many ambitious building projects.

Growing to adulthood in this bastion of liberalism and democracy, Socrates somehow developed a set of values and beliefs that would put him at odds with most of his fellow Athenians. Socrates was not a democrat or an egalitarian. To him, the people should not be self-governing; they were like a herd of sheep that needed the direction of a wise shepherd. He denied that citizens had basic virtue necessary to nurture a good society, instead equating virtue with a knowledge unattainable by ordinary people. Striking at the heart of Athenian democracy, he contemptuously criticised the right of every citizen to speak in the Athenian assembly.

Writing in the third-century C.E. in his *The Lives of Eminent Philosophers*, Diogenes Laertius reported that Socrates "discussed moral questions in the workshops and the marketplace." Often his unpopular views, expressed disdainfully and with an air of condescension, provoked his listeners to anger. Laertius wrote that "men set upon him with their fists or tore his hair out," but Socrates "bore all this ill-usage patiently."

We get one contemporary view of Socrates from playwright Aristophanes. In his play *Clouds*, first produced in 423 B.C.E., Aristophanes presents Socrates as an eccentric and comic headmaster of a "thinkery" (or "thoughtery"). He is portrayed "stalking the streets" of Athens barefoot, "rolling his eyes" at remarks he found unintelligent, and "gazing up" at the clouds. Socrates at the time of *Clouds* must have been perceived more as a harmless town character than as a serious threat to Athenian values and democracy. Socrates himself, apparently, took no offence at his portrayal in *Clouds*. Plutarch, in his *Moralia*, quoted Socrates as saying, "When they break a jest upon me in the theatre, I feel as if I were at a big party of good friends." Plato, in his *Symposium*, describes Socrates and Aristophanes engaged in friendly conversation.

Other plays of the time offer additional clues as to the reputation of Socrates in Athens. Comic poet Eupolis has one of his characters say: "Yes, and I loathe that poverty-stricken windbag Socrates who contemplates everything in the world but does not know where his next meal is coming from." *Birds*, a play of Aristophanes written six years after his *Clouds*, contains a revealing reference. Aristophanes labels a gang of pro-Sparta aristocratic youths as "Socratified." Sparta – the model of a closed society – and Athens were enemies: the remark suggests Socrates' teaching may have started to be seen as subversive by 417 B.C.E.

The standing of Socrates among his fellow citizens suffered mightily during two periods in which Athenian democracy was temporarily overthrown, one for a period of four months in 411-410 and another slightly longer period in 404-403. The prime movers in both of the anti-democratic movements were former pupils of Socrates, Alcibiades and Critias. Athenians undoubtedly considered the teachings of Socrates – especially his expressions of disdain for the established constitution – partially responsible for the resulting death and suffering. Alcibiades, perhaps Socrates' favourite Athenian politician, masterminded the first overthrow. (Alcibiades had other strikes against him: four years earlier, Alcibiades had fled to Sparta to avoid facing trial for mutilating religious pillars – statues of Hermes – and while in Sparta had proposed to the state's leaders that he helped them defeat Athens.) Critias, first among an oligarchy known as the "Thirty Tyrants," led the second bloody revolt against the restored Athenian democracy in 404. The revolt sent many of Athen's leading democratic citizens (including Anytus, later the driving force behind the prosecution of Socrates) into exile, where they organised a resistance movement.

Critias, without question, was the more frightening of the two former pupils of Socrates. I.F. Stone, in his *The Trial of Socrates*, describes Critias (a cousin of Plato's) as "the first Robespierre," a cruel and inhumane man "determined to remake the city to his own antidemocratic mould whatever the human cost." The oligarchy confiscated the estates of Athenian aristocrats, banished 5,000 women, children and slaves, and summarily executed about 1,500 of Athen's most prominent democrats.

One incident involving Socrates and the Thirty Tyrants would later become an issue at his trial. Although the Thirty normally used their own gang of thugs for such duties, the oligarchy asked Socrates to arrest Leon of Salamis so that he might be executed and his assets appropriated. Socrates refused to do so. Socrates would point to his resistance to the order as evidence of his good conduct. On the other hand, Socrates neither protested the decision nor took steps to warn Leon of Salamis of the order for his arrest – he just went home. While good citizens of Athens were being liquidated right and left, Socrates, so far as we know did or said nothing to stop the violence.

The horrors brought on by the Thirty Tyrants caused Athenians to look at Socrates in a new light. His teachings no longer seemed so harmless. He was no longer a lovable town eccentric. Socrates and his icy logic came to be seen as a dangerous and corrupting influence, a breeder of tyrants and enemy of the common man.

Trial

A general amnesty issued in 403 meant that Socrates could not be prosecuted for any of his actions during or before the reign of the Thirty Tyrants. He could only be charged for his actions during the four years preceding his trial in 399 B.C.E. It appears that Socrates, unchastened by the antidemocratic revolts and their aftermaths, resumed his teachings and once again began attracting a similar band of youthful followers. The final straw may well have been an another antidemocratic uprising – this one unsuccessful – in 401. Athens finally had enough of "Socratified" youth.

In Athens, criminal proceedings could be initiated by any citizen. In the case of Socrates, the proceedings began when Meletus, a poet, delivered an oral summons to Socrates in the presence of witnesses. The summons required Socrates to appear before the legal magistrate,

or King Archon, in a colonnaded building in central Athens called the Royal Stoa to answer charges of impiety and corrupting the youth. The Archon determined after listening to Socrates and Meletus (and perhaps the other two accusers, Anytus and Lycon) that the lawsuit was permissible under Athenian law, set a date for the "preliminary hearing" (anakrisis), and posted a public notice at the Royal Stoa.

The preliminary hearing before the magistrate at the Royal Stoa began with the reading of the written charge by Meletus. Socrates answered the charge. The magistrate questioned both Meletus and Socrates, then gave both the accuser and defendant an opportunity to question each other. Having found merit in the accusation against Socrates, the magistrate drew up formal charges. The document containing the charges against Socrates survived until at least the second century C.E. Diogenes Laertius reports the charges as recorded in the now-lost document:

This indictment and affidavit is sworn by Meletus, the son of Meletus of Pitthos, against Socrates, the son of Sophroniscus of Alopece. Socrates is guilty of refusing to recognise the Gods recognised by the state, and of introducing new divinities. He is also guilty of corrupting the youth. The penalty demanded is death.

The trial of Socrates took place over a nine-to-ten hour period in the People's Court, located in the agora, the civic centre of Athens. The jury consisted of 500 male citizens over the age of thirty, chosen by lot. Most of the jurors were farmers. The jurors sat on wooden benches separated from the large crowd of spectators – including a twenty-seven-year-old pupil of Socrates named Plato – by some sort of barrier or railing.

Guilt Phase of Trial

The trial began in the morning with the reading of the formal charges against Socrates by a herald. The prosecution presented its case first. The three accusers, Meletus, Anytus, and Lycon, had a total of three hours, measured by a waterclock, to present from an elevated stage their argument for guilt. No record of the prosecution's argument against Socrates survived.

Easily the best known and most influential of the three accusers, Anytus, is widely believed to have been the driving force behind the prosecution of Socrates. Plato's *Meno* offers a possible clues as to the animosity between Anytus, a politician coming from a family of tanners, and Socrates. In the *Meno*, Plato reports Socrates' argument that the great statesmen of Athenian history have nothing to offer in terms of an understanding of virtue enrages Anytus. Plato quotes Anytus as warning Socrates: "Socrates, I think that you are too ready to speak evil of men and, if you will take my advice, I would recommend you to be careful." Anytus had an additional personal gripe concerning the relationship Socrates had with his son. Plato quotes Socrates as saying, "I had a brief association with the son of Anytus, and I found him not lacking in spirit." It is not known whether the relationship included sex, but Socrates – as were many men of the time in Athens – was bisexual and slept with some of his younger students. Anytus almost certainly disapproved of his son's relationship with Socrates. Adding to the displeasure of Anytus must have been the advice Socrates gave to his son. According to Xenophon, Socrates urged Anytus's son not to "continue in the servile occupation (tanning hides) that his father has provided for him." Without a "worthy adviser," Socrates predicted, he would "fall into some disgraceful propensity and will surely go far in the career of vice."

It is a matter of dispute among historians whether the accusers focused more attention on the alleged religious crimes, or the alleged political crimes of Socrates. I. F. Stone attaches far more significance to the political crimes, while other historians such as James A. Colaiaco, author of *Socrates Against Athens*, give more weight to the charge of impiety.

I. F. Stone argues that Athenians were accustomed to hearing that the Gods were treated disrespectfully in both the comic and tragic theatre. He points out that Aristophanes, in his *Clouds*, had a character speculating that rain was Zeus urinating through a sieve, mistaking it for a chamberpot and that no one ever bothered to charge Aristophanes with impiety. Stone concludes: "One could in the same city and in the same century worship Zeus as a promiscuous old rake, henpecked and cuckolded by Juno or as Justice deified. It was the political, not the philosophical or theological, views of Socrates which finally got him into trouble."

Important support for Stone's conclusion comes from the earliest surviving reference to the trial of Socrates that *does not come from one of his disciples*. In 345 B.C.E., the famous orator Aechines told a jury: "Men of Athens, you executed Socrates, the sophist because he was clearly responsible for the education of Critias, one of the thirty anti-democratic leaders."

James Colaiaco's conclusion that impiety received more prosecutorial attention than did political sins rests on Plato's *Apology*. Colaiaco sees Plato's famous account of the defence of Socrates as being – although far from a verbatim transcription of the words of Socrates – fairly representative of the major points of his defence. He notes that Plato wrote the *Apology* within a few years of the trial and must have expected many of his readers to have firsthand knowledge of the trial. Why, Colaiaco asks, would have Plato misrepresented the arguments of Socrates, or hid key elements of the prosecution's case, when his actions in doing so could so easily be exposed? Since the *Apology* seems to give great weight to the charge of impiety and relatively little weight to the association of Socrates with the Thirty Tyrants, Colaiaco assumes this must have been a fair reflection of the trial. At the same time, Colaiaco recognises that because of the association of Socrates with Critias the prosecution could expect any Athenian jury to harbour hostile feelings toward the city's gadfly.

Piety had, for Athenians, a broad meaning. It included not just respect for the gods, but also for the dead and ancestors. The impious individual was seen as a contaminant who, if not controlled or punished, might bring upon the city the wrath of the Gods – Athena, Zeus, or Apollo – in the form of plague or sterility. The ritualistic religion of Athens included no scripture, church, or priesthood. Rather, it required – in addition to belief in the Gods – observance of rites, prayers, and the offering of sacrifices.

Any number of words and actions of Socrates may have contributed to his impiety charge. Preoccupied with his moral instruction, he probably failed to attend important religious festivals. He may have stirred additional resentment by offering arguments against the collective, ritualistic view of religion shared by most Athenians or by contending that Gods could not, as Athenians believed, behave immorally or whimsically. Xenophon indicates that the impiety charge stemmed primarily from the contention of Socrates that he received divine communications (a "voice" or a "sign") directing him to avoid politics and concentrate on his philosophic mission. A vague charge such as impiety invited jurors to project their many and varied grievances against Socrates.

Dozens of accounts of the three-hour speech (apologia) by Socrates in his defence existed at one time. Only Plato's and Xenophon's accounts survive. The two accounts agree on a key point. Socrates gave a defiant – decidedly *un*apologetic – speech. He seemed to invite condemnation and death.

Plato's apology describes Socrates questioning his accuser, Meletus about the impiety charge. Meletus accuses Socrates of believing the sun and moon not to be Gods, but merely masses of stone. Socrates responds not by specifically denying the charge of atheism, but by attacking Meletus for inconsistency. The charge against him accused him of believing in other Gods, not in believing in no Gods. If Plato's account is accurate, Socrates could have been seen by jurors offering a smokescreen rather than a refutation of the charge of impiety.

Plato's Socrates provocatively tells his jury that he is a hero. He reminds them of his exemplary service as a hoplite in three battles. More importantly, he contends, he has battled for decades to save the souls of Athenians – pointing them in the direction of an examined, ethical life. He reportedly says to his jurors that if his teaching about the nature of virtue corrupts the youth, he is a mischievous person. He tells the jury, according to Plato, he would rather be put to death than give up his soul-saving: "Men of Athens, I honour and love you; but I shall obey God rather than you, and while I have life and strength I shall never cease from the practice and teaching of philosophy." If Plato's account is accurate, the jury knew that the only way to stop Socrates from lecturing about the moral weaknesses of Athenians was to kill him.

If I. F. Stone is right, the most damaging accusation against Socrates concerned his association with Critias, the cruel leader of the Thirty Tyrants. Socrates, in Plato's account, points to his refusal to comply with the Tyrants' order that he bring in Leon of Salamis for summary execution. He argues this act of disobedience – which might have led to his own execution, had not the Tyrants fallen from power – demonstrates his service as a good citizen of Athens. Stone notes, however, that a good citizen might have done more than simply go home to bed – he might have warned Leon of Salamis. In Stone's critical view, the central fact remained that in the city's darkest hour, Socrates "never shed a tear for Athens." As for the charge that his moral instruction provided intellectual cover for the anti-democratic revolt of Critias and his cohorts, Socrates denies responsibility. He argues that he never presumed to be a teacher, just a figure who roamed Athens answering the questions that were put to him. He points to his pupils in the crowd and observes that none of them accused him. Moreover, Socrates suggests to the jury, if Critias really understood his words, he never would have gone on the bloody rampage that he did in 404-403. Hannah Arendt notes that Critias apparently concluded, from the message of Socrates that piety cannot be defined, that it is permissible to be impious – pretty much the opposite of what Socrates had hoped to achieve by talking about piety.

What is strikingly absent from the defence of Socrates, if Plato's and Xenophon's accounts are to be believed, is the plea for mercy typically made to Athenian juries. It was common practice to appeal to the sympathies of jurors by introducing wives and children. Socrates, however, did no more than remind the jury that he had a family. Neither his wife, Xanthippe nor any of his three sons made a personal appearance. On the contrary, Socrates, according to Plato contends that the unmanly and pathetic practice of pleading for clemency disgraces the justice system of Athens.

When the three-hour defence of Socrates came to an end, the court herald asked the jurors to render their decision by putting their ballot disks in one of two marked urns, one for guilty votes and one for votes for acquittal. With no judge to offer them instructions as to how to interpret the charges or the law, each juror struggled with oneself to come to an understanding of the case and the guilt or innocence of Socrates. When the ballots were counted, 280 jurors had voted to find Socrates guilty, 220 jurors for acquittal.

Penalty Phase of Trial

After the conviction of Socrates by a relatively close vote, the trial entered its penalty phase. Each side, the accusers and the defendant, was given an opportunity to propose a punishment. After listening to arguments, the jurors would choose which of the two proposed punishments to adopt.

The accusers of Socrates proposed the punishment of death. In proposing death, the accusers might well have expected to counter with a proposal for exile – a punishment that probably would have satisfied both them and the jury. Instead, Socrates audaciously proposes to the jury that he be rewarded, not punished. According to Plato, Socrates asks the jury for free meals in the Prytaneum, a public dining hall in the centre of Athens. Socrates must have known that his proposed "punishment" would infuriate the jury. I. F. Stone noted that Socrates acts more like a picador trying to enrage a bull than a defendant trying to mollify a jury. Why, then, propose a punishment guaranteed to be rejected? The only answer, Stone and others conclude, is that Socrates was ready to die.

To comply with the demand that a genuine punishment be proposed, Socrates reluctantly suggested a fine of one mina of silver – about one-fifth of his modest net worth, according to Xenophon. Plato and other supporters of Socrates upped the offer to thirty minae by agreeing to come up with silver of their own. Most jurors likely believed even the heftier fine to be far too slight of a punishment for the unrepentant defendant.

In the final vote, a larger majority of jurors favoured a punishment of death than voted in the first instance for conviction. According to Diogenes Laertius, 360 jurors voted for death, 140 for the fine. Under Athenian law, execution was accomplished by drinking a cup of poisoned hemlock.

In Plato's *Apology*, the trial concludes with Socrates offering a few memorable words as court officials finished their necessary work. He tells the crowd that his conviction resulted from his unwillingness to address them as they would have liked him to do. He predicts that history will come to see his conviction as "shameful for Athens," though he professes to have no ill will for the jurors who convict him. Finally, as he is being led off to jail, Socrates utters the memorable line: "The hour of departure has arrived, and we go our ways – I to die, and you to live. Which to the better fate is known only to God." It is likely that this last burst of eloquence comes from Plato, not Socrates. There are no records suggesting that Athenian practice allowed defendants to speak after sentencing.

Socrates spent his final hours in a cell in the Athens jail. The ruins of the jail remain today. The hemlock that ended his life did not do so quickly or painlessly, but rather by producing a gradual paralysis of the central nervous system.

Most scholars see the conviction and execution of Socrates as a deliberate choice made by the famous philosopher himself. If the accounts of Plato and Xenophon are reasonably accurate, Socrates sought not to persuade jurors, but rather to lecture and provoke them.

The trial of Socrates, the most interesting suicide the world has ever seen, produced the first martyr for free speech. As I. F. Stone observed, just as Jesus needed the cross to fulfill his mission, Socrates needed his hemlock to fulfill his.

Socrates

Born: c. 469, Athens

Died: 399 B.C.E., Athens

Greek philosopher whose way of life, character, and thought exerted a profound influence on ancient and modern philosophy.

Because he wrote nothing, information about his personality and doctrine is derived chiefly from depictions of his conversations and other information in the dialogues of Plato, in the Memorabilia of Xenophon, and in various writings of Aristotle. He fought bravely in the Peloponnesian War and later served in the Athenian boule (assembly). Socrates considered it his religious duty to call his fellow citizens to the examined life by engaging them in philosophical conversation. His contribution to these exchanges typically consisted of a series of probing questions that cumulatively revealed his interlocutor's complete ignorance of the subject under discussion; such cross-examination used as a pedagogical technique has been called the "Socratic method." Though Socrates characteristically professed his own ignorance regarding many of the (mainly ethical) subjects he investigated (e.g., the nature of piety), he did hold certain convictions with confidence, including that: (1) human wisdom begins with the recognition of one's own ignorance; (2) the unexamined life is not worth living; (3) ethical virtue is the only thing that matters; and (4) a good person can never be harmed, because whatever misfortune he may suffer, his virtue will remain intact. His students and admirers included, in addition to Plato, Alcibiades, who betrayed Athens in the Peloponnesian War, and Critias (c. 480–403 BC), who was one of the Thirty Tyrants imposed on Athens after its defeat by Sparta. Because he was connected with these two men, but also because his habit of exposing the ignorance of his fellow citizens had made him widely hated and feared, Socrates was tried on charges of impiety and corrupting the youth and condemned to death by poisoning (the poison probably being hemlock) in 399 BC; he submitted to the sentence willingly. Plato's Apology purports to be the speech that Socrates gave in his own defence. As depicted in the Apology, Socrates' trial and death raise vital questions about the nature of democracy, the value of free speech, and the potential conflict between moral and religious obligation and the laws of the state.

6. The Trial of *Jesus*

Providing an account of the trial of Jesus presents challenges unlike any of the other trials on the Famous Trials. First, there is the challenge of determining what actually happened nearly 2,000 years ago before the Sanhedrin and the Roman prefect of Judea, Pontius Pilate. The task is daunting because almost our entire understanding of events comes from five divergent accounts, each of which was written by a Christian (who did not witness the final days of Jesus directly) for a distinct audience from fifteen (at least) to seventy years after the trial. Second, there is the challenge that comes from knowing that readers of this account are likely to have prior understandings of trial events that come from their own religious training and that any account of the trial provided here that varies substantially from these prior understandings may not be easily accepted. Nonetheless, I believe the trial of Jesus merits analysis for the simple reason that no other trial in human history has so significantly affected the course of human events.

The Setting

In 63 B.C.E. the Roman general Pompey captured Jerusalem, and in doing so put an end both to the independent Jewish state of Palestine and eight decades of rule by the Hasmonean dynasty of high priests. Rome began appointing the high priests that served the Temple in Jerusalem. High priests from then on juggled the religious interests of Jews and the political interests of Rome, at whose pleasure they served.

Seven decades after Rome assumed control of Palestine, in 6 C.E., growing Jewish opposition to Roman laws relating to the census, taxation, and heathen traditions boiled over. Especially despised was the Roman imposition of a census of property for tax purposes. Ancestral land held an exalted position in Jewish ideology and many Jews feared that the new laws would lead to its appropriation by Rome. Jewish uprisings in protest of the laws led to the crucifixion of over 2,000 Jewish insurgents and the selling into slavery of perhaps 20,000 more. The most intense opposition to Rome came from an area of Palestine called Galilee, which was the centre of an armed resistance movement called the Zealots.

The riots of 6 C.E. and recurring outbreaks that followed caused Roman officials to see Jewish nationalism and religious fervour as threatening to law and order. When Herod Antipas, the Roman ruler of Galilee, constructed a new capital city, Tiberius, on the western shore of Galilee in 19 C.E., he might have expected trouble from the peasant population forced to meet heavier tax burdens to pay for it. In any event, trouble came, as two significant Jewish religious movements were born in the next decade in the region of northern Palestine under his rule.

The first important movement to arise in Galilee was led by the apocalyptic visionary, John the Baptist. The Baptist called upon his followers to confess their sins, live an ascetic lifestyle, and prepare for the imminent coming of an avenging God. To the purification process offered in the Temple, he presented a radical new alternative: a ritual immersion in the waters of the Jordan River.

John the Baptist's growing popularity among the peasant population alarmed Herod Antipas, who likely feared that the new movement, with its promise of apocalyptic intervention could lead to rioting. Antipas made a preemptive strike. He arrested and executed, according to Biblical accounts the Baptist. The execution of John the Baptist may have deeply influenced one of his early disciples, a young man from Nazareth that he had baptised in the Jordan river (Mark 1:9-11), Jesus.

The execution of John the Baptist is likely to have had a profound effect on Jesus. God's non-intervention might have caused Jesus to modify the apocalyptic vision of John the Baptist which was probably a product of the perceived hopelessness of the peasants' plight to one that emphasised change in the structure of political and religious institutions. The teachings of Jesus, who began his ministry around 28 or 29 C.E., describe an ideal world, a world that might exist if God and not Caesar or the high priests had his way. Jesus spoke primarily of the need to change the here and now, and less of need to ready oneself for the arrival of an avenging God. Needless to say, a religious program of the sort presented by Jesus would likely be seen as threatening by powerful beneficiaries of the status quo, from Roman leaders to Temple officials.

Antipas might well have preferred Jesus dead, but he had to balance that desire against popular resentment related to his execution of the popular John the Baptist. For that reason or some other, Antipas did not move to suppress the Kingdom of God movement led by Jesus.

The Crime

To understand the crime which likely led to the arrest of Jesus, it is first necessary to understand the role of the Temple in first-century

Jewish life. The Temple in Jerusalem served dual purposes. It was both the revered centre of religious life – a place for prayers and sacrifices and a central bank, a place for taxes and tithes.

Nothing provoked greater anger among observant Jews than acts perceived to be defilements of the Temple, as other dramatic incidents in the two decades following the death of Jesus make clear. In 41 C.E. for example, Emperor Caligula ordered Petronius, the new

Syrian governor to install statues in the Temple depicting himself as Zeus incarnate. Thousands of unarmed Jews responded by lying prostrate and offering themselves to Roman soldiers for a mass slaughter. Other Jews threatened an agricultural strike. Petronius backed down and Caligula's timely assassination ended the matter. Less than ten years later, a soldier watching over Jews celebrating the Passover at the Temple (according to historian Josephus, writing in about 90 C.E.) raised his robe, stooped in an indecent attitude, so as to turn his backside to the Jews, and made a noise in keeping with his posture. This disrespectful gesture led to a riot and stampede that killed vast numbers of people – "Troops pouring into the porticoes, the Jews were seized with irresistible panic and turned to fly from the Temple and make their escape into town. But such violence as was used as they pressed around the exits that they were trodden under foot and crushed to death by one another; upwards of 30,000 perished, and the feast was turned into mourning for the whole nation and for every household into lamentation." (Josephus, *Jewish Antiquities*)

Roman leaders paid close attention to Temple activity. Any threat to Roman power over the Temple even a symbolic threat was dealt with harshly, as seen by the response to an incident around 5 B.C.E. When a group of about forty young men climbed to the roof of the Temple and began chopping down a golden eagle, seen by them as a symbol of Roman control, the men were (according to Josephus) arrested "with considerable force." Those observed on the Temple roof were burnt alive and the others merely executed.

It seems clear that the primary cause of the trial and execution of Jesus was his role in an incident at the Temple in Jerusalem. The incident occurred in April, 30 C.E. (or possibly in 33 C.E.) during Festival time, the period including the Day of Passover leading into the week of the Unleavened Bread. The Festival brought huge numbers of Jews into the city to celebrate the Exodus, the leaving of Egyptian oppression and the arrival in the Promised Land. Romans had to understand the special risks presented by such a commemoration. There were large concentrations of Jews celebrating their former freedom in a time of new oppression – this time by Rome, not Egypt.

Jesus probably came to Jerusalem about a week before the Passover, most likely for the purpose of carrying his message of the imminent coming of the Kingdom of God into the heart of Israel – though possibly, like so many thousands of other Jews, simply to celebrate the highest of religious days.

Gospel accounts describe the participation of Jesus in a protest directed at some of the commercial practices associated with the Temple. The practices offended many Jews. According to Matthew, Jesus had complained, "My house shall be called a house of prayer, but you have made it a den of robbers" (Matthew 21:13). Mark and John tell of Jesus overturning the tables of money-changers, those persons who converted coins bearing images of the emperor into Tyrian silver coins, the only form of coin acceptable for donations. The Gospels also describe Jesus driving the pigeon-sellers (the birds were used as sacrifices by worshipers) from the Temple. It is hard to imagine that such a dramatic action would not have brought an immediate response from armed Temple guards, so it is likely that the gospels exaggerated Jesus' actions. Whatever the precise nature of his actions, they were almost certainly accompanied by words, perhaps including a prediction that the Temple would fall unless reforms were instituted to bring the Temple back to its central religious mission.

At a time of high tension such as the Passover festival, it is likely that any subversive action in the Temple, even action of a symbolic nature would provoke a strong response from high priests and Roman officials. It did.

Arrest and Trial

The four gospels place the time and scene of the arrest of Jesus as night in the garden of Gethsemane, an olive grove just west of Jerusalem on the Mount of Olives. The arresting party most likely consisted of Temple police dispatched by Caiaphas, the high priest. The party may also have included, as John reports, a Roman cohort under its commanding officer, but it is hard to believe that deployment of so large a force (a cohort consisted of about 600 men) would be seen as desirable to effectuate the arrest of a single individual.

The role in the arrest of Jesus of Judas, a follower of Jesus, is a matter of historical debate. Jesus Scholar Bart Ehrman, author of *Jesus: Apocalyptic Prophet of the New Millenium*, notes that prior to the disturbance at the Temple, nothing Jesus had said suggested he

thought himself the Messiah or King of the Jews. Asking the question, "So where did the authorities get the idea that he did?" Erhman suggests an answer: Judas. As a motive for his betrayal, Erhman identifies two theories. The first theory holds that Judas became disillusioned when he realised that Jesus had no intention of assuming the role of a political-military Messiah. The second theory holds that Judas wanted to force Jesus' hand and believed that his arrest would lead to a call for an uprising against Roman rule. Other scholars such as John Crossan, author of *Who Killed Jesus?* have a somewhat simpler explanation. Crossan speculates that Judas may have been captured in the incident at the Temple – and that he might have been pressured to tell authorities *who* had caused the Temple trouble, not just where the guilty party might be found.

The gospels provide three very different accounts of the trial of Jesus. Peter, possibly writing as early as the 40s C.E. describes a single trial scene involving Jewish, Roman, and Herodian officials. Mark, writing in the 60s C.E. describes two separate proceedings, one involving Jewish leaders and the other in which the Roman prefect for Judea, Pontius Pilate plays the key role. Matthew and John's account generally support Mark's two-trial version. Finally, Luke alone among the gospels adds a third proceeding, having Pilate pass the buck (for jurisdictional reasons) and sending Jesus to Herod Antipas.

Figuring out what really happened in the trial of Jesus is enormously difficult. Two surviving non-Christian accounts, one by Roman historian and another by a Jewish historian, confirm that Pilate ordered the execution of Jesus but beyond that, offer few details. Writing in the late first-century, Tacitus offered this comment:

Christus (Jesus), from whom the name had its origin, suffered the extreme penalty during the reign of Tiberius at the hands of one of our procurators, Pontius Pilate, and a most mischievous superstition, thus checked for the moment, again broke out not only in Judaea, and the first source of the evil, but even in Rome, where all things hideous and shameful from every part of the world find their centre and become popular.

The Jewish historian, Flavius Josephus, writing in the 80s or early 90s C.E., indicated that both Jewish leaders and the Roman prefect played roles in the crucifixion of Jesus:

About the same time there lived Jesus, a wise man for he was a performer of marvelous feats and a teacher of such men who received the truth with pleasure. He attracted many Jews and many Greeks. He was called the Christ. Pilate sentenced him to die on the cross, having been urged to do so by the noblest of our citizens; but those who loved him at first did not give up their affection for him. And the tribe of the Christians, who are named after him, have not disappeared to this day.

Josephus would have no reason to attribute a non-existent role to the noblest of our citizens, so it is probably safe to assume that Jewish leaders did encourage Pilate to crucify Jesus. Questions remain, however, as to what form that encouragement took and how willingly or unwillingly Pilate responded to their encouragement.

The gospels report that Jesus was brought before high priest Joseph Caiaphas and the Sanhedrin, the Jewish supreme governing council and court. Mark and Matthew report a trial at night in the house of Caiaphas, whereas Luke explicitly states that Jesus was tried in the morning before the Sanhedrin. Some scholars doubt the accuracy of of the gospel accounts. They note that Jewish law prohibits both capital trials on the eves of a festival and trials by night. Other scholars answer that Jewish law might have been different then.

The gospels point to different sources of initial concern among the Jewish authorities. Mark suggests that the Jewish authorities were concerned primarily with the confrontation Jesus had with traders in the Temple, while Luke's account identifies their primary concern as his teachings in the Temple. John, meanwhile, points to a fear among Jewish authorities that Jesus' rising popularity could lead to an uprising that would provoke a violent response from Rome.

All four Biblical accounts agree, however, that Caiaphas and the Sanhedrin ultimately condemned Jesus for blasphemy. The gospels record that when Caiaphas asked Jesus whether he claimed to be the Messiah, he replied, "I am" (Mark 14:62) (or "You have said so" (Matthew 26:64) or "If I tell you, you will not believe" (Luke 22:67-8) or "You say that I am" (John 19:7)). Although the Mishnah, the Jewish lawcode assembled around 200 C.E., defined blasphemy more narrowly as speaking the sacred name of God (YHWH), the gospel writers suggest a looser first-century construction of the term, one that includes a variety of serious theological offenses.

After his condemnation by Jewish authorities, Jesus was brought under all but Peter's account to the Roman prefect of Judea, Pontius Pilate. The reason, according to John, was that the death penalty was not an available option for the Sanhedrin under Roman law. (It should be noted, however, that the Sanhedrin operated during these times with less than complete independence to implement Jewish law, having a dual political and religious status.) There is, however, strong reason to believe that Jewish authorities could, had they so desired, executed Jesus. The well-substantiated executions by stoning of two first-century Christians, Jesus's brother James in 62 C.E. and Stephen, show that capital punishment was at least within a few decades of Jesus' trial practiced by Jewish authorities. Moreover, Temple inscriptions from the period warn of death to Gentiles that pass into certain restricted areas.

Biblical accounts of the trial before Pilate are largely fictional, according to most scholars. It is unlikely that any supporter of Christ would have been in a position to record any questioning of Jesus by Pilate that might have taken place.

Whatever their basis, the gospels portray a Pilate initially unpersuaded of Jesus' guilt. For example, in Mark, after Pilate asks Jesus about "the many charges (the chief priests) bring against you," Jesus makes "no further answer" and "Pilate wondered." Later, Mark reinforces his suggestion of a reluctant executioner when he writes, "For Pilate perceived that it was out of envy that the chief priests had delivered him up." Finally, Mark makes Pilate's doubts explicit by having him almost beg the crowd to release Jesus over the (almost certainly invented) prisoner Barabbas. Pilate asks the crowd to explain their thirst for the blood of Jesus: "Why, what evil has he done?" Pilate allows the crucifixion of Jesus, in the gospel accounts, not out of a conviction that Jesus did anything wrong, but only to satisfy the crowd. If there were still any doubt about Pilate's doubt, the gospels report that after authorising his execution, he washes his hands.

The gospel accounts so transparently attempt to present the chief priests and not Pilate as the more blameworthy party that scholars have raised numerous questions about their accuracy. Scholars have paid special attention to the incentives of Mark because he wrote the earliest of the four gospel accounts in the Bible, and Matthew, Luke, and (to a lesser extent) John based their accounts on his. The scholars point out that Mark writing at a time of Roman prosecution of Christians and for a largely non-Jewish audience had incentives to present a story that would minimise the risk of condemnation by Roman authorities and maximise his prospects for winning converts to Christianity from among the Romans in his audience. How could Mark, these scholars ask, possibly have known what Pilate "wondered" about Jesus' guilt or what he "perceived" about the purposes of high priests?

Pilate was a powerful figure. If he had reservations about killing Jesus, he certainly could have taken him back to Caesaria for trial or referred his case back to the Sanhedrin for possible punishment under Jewish, not Roman, law. The fact that Pilate did not do so suggests that he was pleased to accede to the urgings of Jewish leaders and crucify Jesus. Anyone calling himself "King of the Jews" would have been seen as trouble by Roman officials. Further evidence that Pilate bore primary responsibility for the execution of Jesus comes from Paul in his letter to the Corinthians, written in the early 50s C.E., where he says that Jesus had been crucified by "the princes of the world"(I Cor. 2:8).

It is altogether possible that there not only was no trial before the Sanhedrin, but none before Pilate either. Pilate and Caiaphus worked long – and probably therefore – and well together. They very likely might have had standing arrangements for dealing with subversive action during festival time. These arrangements could have included, according to Biblical scholar John Crossan, "instant punishment with immediate crucifixion as public warning and deterrent." Crossan argues, "There would be no need to go very high up the chain of command for a nuisance nobody like Jesus, no need even for a formal interrogation before Caiaphas, let alone a detailed trial before Pilate." Ehrman agrees, writing, "If someone was perceived to be a troublemaker, there was no need to follow anything that would strike us as due process, at leat for the non-Roman citizens of the provinces." Ehrman adds, "There would have been no reason to conduct a criminal investigation out in the open and ask for the crowds' opinions."

Pilate had little concern for Jewish sensibilities. During his ten-year tenure (from 26 C.E. to 36 C.E.) as prefect, Pilate had numerous confrontations with his Jewish subjects. According to Jewish historian Josephus, Pilate's decision to bring into the holy city of Jerusalem "by night and under cover effigies of Caesar" outraged Jews who considered the images idolatrous. Pilate provoked another outcry from his Jewish subjects when he used Temple funds to build an aqueduct. His lack of feeling was accompanied, according to Jewish philosopher Philo writing in 41 C.E., by corruption and brutality. Philo wrote that Pilate's tenure was associated with "briberies, insults, robberies, outrages, wanton injustices, constantly repeated executions without trial, and ceaseless and grievous cruelty." Philo may have overstated the case, but there is little to suggest that Pilate would have any serious reservations about executing a Jewish rabble-rouser such as Jesus.

Crucifixion

In some particulars, Biblical accounts of Jesus's punishment are consistent with what would be expected under first-century Roman law. Most obviously, the form of execution used – crucifixion – was a common one at the time when the convicted criminal was a slave, Jew, or other foreigner. (Romans were exempt from crucifixion, which was thought to be the most painful and humiliating of all punishments.) Crucifixion also establishes conclusively that Jesus was condemned as a violator of Roman, not Jewish, law. A capital sentence under Jewish law would have meant stoning.

Other aspects of the Biblical accounts of the execution that match common Roman practice include the flogging Jesus received at the hand of Roman soldiers before his execution, his carrying of the cross to the place of execution, and the guarding of the execution site by a unit of four Roman soldiers. The execution site identified in the gospels, Golgotha (meaning "place of the skull" in Aramaic), is probably accurate; although which of two possible hillsides north of Jerusalem might have been "Golgotha" is a matter of current dispute.

Unfortunately, horrific details of the crucifixion account, such as the nailing of the hands and feet of Jesus to the cross, also are probably true. In 1968, a nail-pierced heel bone of a first-century crucifixion victim was found near Jerusalem providing fresh evidence of Roman cruelty. The stripping of prisoners seems also to have been standard Roman practice, with the clothes and other small possessions of execution victims divided among the executioners. The humiliation of being hanged nude in a prominent place added to the punishment's intended deterrent value.

The Gospel of John reports that the Jews did not want the bodies left on the cross during the sabbath...so they asked Pilate to have the legs of the crucified men broken. This reference, obscure to most modern readers, is to what was considered a merciful act. Crucifixion is normally a painful and long death, with victims sometimes remaining alive on the cross for days. Leg breaking speeds the process by causing a rapid onset of asphyxiation or fatal shock. John's account indicates that Jesus was already dead when the soldiers arrived to break his legs. That may indeed have been the case, but Jesus' reportedly quick death accounts vary from about three hours in John to six hours in Mark would have been unusual.

Many other details in the gospel accounts appear to be added by early Christian writers to show the passion story as a fulfillment of Old Testament prophesies concerning the coming of Messiah. For example, four accounts (Mark, Matthew, Luke, and Peter) describe a three-hour period of darkness falling over the land beginning at noon on the day of crucifixion of Jesus. Luke refers specifically to a solar eclipse that lasted until three in the afternoon. It is possible to calculate backwards the dates and locations of solar eclipses, and it is clear that no eclipse occurred in Jerusalem at the time of the crucifixion. It is also clear from other sources that solar eclipses were, in the first-century, associated with human events of great significance. Josephus, Plutarch, and Pliny the Elder each report, for example, that midday darkness followed the assassination of Julius Caesar on March 15, 44 B.C.E. – although, again, it did not. Thus, a writer seeking to impress readers that the crucifixion of Jesus was the fulfillment of a historic prophesy would have been tempted to add the fictional element of a solar eclipse to his account. The reported words of Jesus on the cross are believed to also fall into the category of prophesy historicised rather than history remembered.

Several early sources indicate that crucifixion victims were typically left on their crosses, their bodies to be eaten by vultures and dogs. Friends of Jesus would have preferred a kinder fate for him, and it is possible that some of his supporters, or Jewish religious authorities believing "enough is enough," succeeded in obtaining permission to remove Jesus from his cross. If this happened, he likely would have been buried in a rock tomb, most likely one belonging to his family. It is also possible, however, that what happened to the body of Jesus is what happened to most victims of Roman crucifixions – it *was* devoured on the cross by animals. John Crossan, author of *Who Killed Jesus?* finds the latter outcome the more likely:

"I keep thinking of all those thousands of Jews crucified around Jerusalem in the terrible first century from among whom we have found only one skeleton and one nail. I think I know what happened to their bodies, and I have no reason to believe that Jesus' body did not join them... The burial stories are hope and hyperbole expanded into apologetics and polemics. But hope is not always history, and neither is hyperbole. In this case, as so often before and after, horror is history."

The Aftermath

Within six years of the crucifixion of Jesus, Syrian governor Vitellius removed from power both of the men – Joseph Caiaphas and Pontius Pilate – most responsible for his execution. Pilate's repeated difficulties with his Jewish subjects was the apparent cause for Vitellius' decision to remove him. Rome ordered Pilate home to face complaints of excessive cruelty, which eventually led to his exile in Vienne, France.

Meanwhile, the followers of Jesus began to split into two branches. One branch, based in Jerusalem and led by the brother of Jesus, James, portrayed Jesus as a martyr for Jewish nationalism. The other branch, the so-called "Gentile branch," was led by the Apostle Paul who rejected the historical Jesus and largely created the version of Jesus found in the Bible today. In place of the historical Jesus, Paul who had relatively little knowledge of the real Jesus substituted a heavenly redeemer who emphasised transformation through love and inward faith. Paul spread his message among the Gentiles, winning converts to his brand of Christianity which did not require full observance of traditional Jewish law.

While the very earliest Christian writings saw the trial and execution of Jesus as the rejection of the Messiah, soon writings began portraying the execution has having a deeper meaning. It was part of God's plan to save humanity as prophesied in writings now comprising the Old Testament.

In 62 C.E., James was stoned to death. Eight years later, Rome captured and destroyed Jerusalem marking the end of the four-year First Jewish War. The "Jerusalem branch" of Jewish Christianity was effectively crushed (although small sects survived until around 300 C.E.), leaving Paul's "Gentile branch" as the Christian torch-carrier.

Over the next twenty-five years, the four Biblical passion accounts were written. Marks' version came first, and the Gospels of Matthew and Luke derived largely from his. John's version was written last, probably around 80 to 95 C.E. John, too, relied heavily on Mark, but is much more creative in his presentation than Matthew or Luke. All three non-Markan gospels also rely, most likely, on a now-lost second account of the trial and crucifixion story.

Most significantly, all four Gospel accounts, written to appeal the Gentiles in Rome and elsewhere, manipulate their stories to make Jewish authorities – not Roman authorities – primarily responsible for Christ's death. In so doing, these early Christian writers undoubtedly contributed to the growth of anti-Semitism with all of its tragic consequences. They also, however, made possible the long-term survival of the Christian faith, with all of its positive messages of love, hope, and faith.

Jesus

In Christianity, Jesus is the son of God and the second person of the Holy Trinity.

Christian doctrine holds that by his crucifixion and resurrection he paid for the sins of all mankind. His life and ministry are recounted in the four Gospels of the New Testament. He was born a Jew in Bethlehem before the death of Herod the Great in 4 BC, and he died while Pontius Pilate was Roman governor of Judaea (AD 28–30). His mother, Mary, was married to Joseph, a carpenter of Nazareth. Of his childhood after the birth narratives in Matthew and Luke, nothing is known, except for one visit to Jerusalem with his parents. He began his ministry about age 30, become a preacher, teacher, and healer. He gathered disciples in the region of Galilee, including the 12 Apostles, and preached the imminent arrival of the Kingdom of God. His moral teachings, outlined in the Sermon on the Mount, and his reported miracles won him a growing number of followers, who believed that he was the promised Messiah. On Passover he entered Jerusalem on a donkey, where he shared the Last Supper with his disciples and was betrayed to the Roman authorities by Judas Iscariot. Arrested and tried, he was condemned to death as a political agitator and was crucified and buried. Three days later visitors to his tomb found it empty. According to the Gospels, he appeared several times to his disciples before ascending into heaven.

7. The Trial of *Martin Luther*

Historians have described it as the trial that led to the birth of the modern world. Before the emperor of the Holy Roman Empire and the Diet of Worms in the spring of 1521, as Luther biographer Roland H. Bainton noted, "The past and the future were met." Martin Luther bravely defended his written attacks on orthodox Catholic beliefs and denied the power of Rome to determine what is right and wrong in matters of faith. By holding steadfast to his interpretation of Scripture, Luther provided the impetus for the Reformation, a reform movement that would divide Europe into two regions, one Protestant and one Catholic, and that would set the scene for religious wars that would continue for more than a century, not ending until the Peace of Westphalia in 1648.

Martin Luther's long journey to Worms might be said to have begun in 1505 on a road near his home town of Erfurt in Saxony (now part of Germany), when a bolt of lightening knocked Luther to the ground. Luther took the lightening to be a call from God, and to the disappointment of his father, who hoped he would become a lawyer, took vows at an Augustinian monastery to begin a profoundly Christian life. Luther impressed his superiors at the Erfurt monastery. By 1507, he was an ordained priest and had offered his first mass. By 1508, he had earned a degree in Biblical studies from the University of Wittenberg and become an instructor at that Augustinian institution.

Questioning the Sale of Indulgences

A trip to Rome in 1510 caused Luther to seriously question certain Catholic practices. The opportunity for the trip arose when Luther was selected as one of two Augustinian brothers to travel to the Eternal City to help resolve a dispute within the order that called for resolution by the Pope. What Luther saw in Rome disillusioned him.

As he watched incompetent, flippant, and cynical clergy performing their holy duties, he began to experience doubts about the Catholic Church. He wrote after his journey that he had gone with onions and returned with garlic.

Those early doubts concerning Rome and its ways would blossom over the next several years after Luther earned the prestigious post as Doctor of the Bible at Wittenberg University and undertook a thorough review of the source book of his religion. Luther's study led him to the theology of Paul and his belief in the possibility of forgiveness through faith made possible by the crucifixion of Christ. In Paul's theology, which Luther would largely adopt as his own, there was no need to look to priests for forgiveness because, to those who believed and were contrite, forgiveness was a gift of God.

Luther's understanding of Paul's theology led him to view skeptically the Catholic Church's reliance on the practice of selling indulgences as its major source of revenue. (An indulgence was a remission of temporal punishment after a confessor revealed sin, expressed contrition, and made the required contribution to the Church.) In sermons in Wittenberg beginning in 1516, Luther argued that forgiveness came from within, and that no one whether a priest or a Pope was in position to grant forgiveness because no one can look into the soul of another. He also questioned whether the Pope could, as he claimed, deliver souls of a confessor's dead loved ones from purgatory. By lashing out at the sale of indulgences, Luther was striking at the heart of the Church's array of money-raising tools and confrontation was inevitable.

Matters began to come to a head the next year when Pope Leo X launched an indulgence-driven campaign to raise funds for construction of a grand basilica of St. Peter's in Rome. The practice of the time was to grant the privilege of selling indulgences to various bishops, who would retain for themselves and their purposes a portion of the raised funds. Albert of Brandenburg, granted an indulgence franchise in his territory for eight years, told his indulgence vendors that they could promise purchasers a perfect remission of all sins and that those seeking indulgences for dead relatives need not be contrite themselves, nor confess their sins. Proclamation of the indulgence fell to an experienced Dominican vendor named John Tetzel, who journeyed from town to town around Albert's territories. Tetzel would follow a cross bearing the papal arms into a town's marketplace and launch into a sermon, or sales pitch, that included a jingle that Martin Luther found especially objectionable:

As soon as the coin in the coffer rings,
The soul from purgatory springs.

Luther, in an angry response to the indulgence sales campaign, prepared in Latin a placard consisting of *Ninety-Five Theses* for debate. The placard, in accordance with the custom of the time, was placed upon the door of Wittenberg's Castle Church. The power of pardon, Luther contended in his *Ninety-Five Theses*, was God alone. If, indeed, the Pope had the power he claimed, Luther asked why he didn't simply exercise it: "If the Pope does have the power to release anyone from purgatory, why in the name of love does he not abolish purgatory by letting everyone out?" Luther's complaints also went to the Church's justification for promoting contributions. He complained about the revenues of all Christendom being sucked into this insatiable basilica when their were much greater needs, including living temples and local churches.

When a copy of Luther's theses reached Rome, the Pope, according to some accounts, said: "Luther is a drunken German. He will feel different when he is sober." Nonetheless, the Pope saw Luther as sufficiently threatening to appoint a new general of the Augustinian order in the hopes that the he would smother the fire before it should become a conflagration. Surprisingly, however, at the gathering of Luther's chapter that year in Heidelberg, Luther's arguments met with enthusiasm among the younger Augustinians and mere head-shaking among the older attendees.

Encouraged by the reception to his views, Luther aimed at new targets. He challenged the power of the Church to excommunicate its members, writing that only God could sever spiritual communion. He also questioned the primacy of the Church in Rome, suggesting that there was a lack of historical support for putting its authority above that of other churches. Clearly, the Pope began to understand, Luther was more of a threat that he first thought. The Pope turned to Dominican Sylvester Prierias, Master of the Sacred Palace at Rome, to draft a reply to Luther's arguments. Prierias's reply branded Luther a heretic and, gratuitously, called him "a leper with a brain of brass and a nose of iron." On August 7, 1518, Luther received a citation to appear in Rome to answer the charge of heresy.

The Road to Worms

Frederick the Wise, the Elector for Germany in the Holy Roman Empire, found himself in the middle of an unwanted controversy. From Pope Leo, Frederick had received a letter expressing concern that had provided support for Martin Luther, a son of iniquity who had been hurling himself upon the Church of God. The Pope called upon Frederick to place Luther in the hands of the Holy See lest future generations reproach you with having fostered the rise of a most pernicious heresy against the Church. Feeling obligations to the Church but also somewhat sympathetic to Luther, whose attacks on Rome won substantial support in his home region, Frederick sought a compromise. In negotiations with Cardinal Cajetan, the papal legate, Frederick prevailed in having Luther's hearing on the heresy charge moved to Augsburg, a city on German soil.

Cardinal Cajetan interviewed Luther three times from October 12-14, 1518. Told that he must recant his views on indulgences and papal infallibility, Luther refuses. On the issue of papal infallibility, Luther said, "I deny that he is above scripture." The frustrated cardinal complained after the meeting with Luther's superior, John Staupitz, "His eyes are as deep as a lake, and there are amazing speculations in his head." Luther remained in Augsburg for another week awaiting some sort of decision from the Church, but when rumours reach him of a plan to have him arrested, he fled on horseback at night.

Catejan pressured Frederick the Wise to have Luther either arrested and sent to Rome or banished from his territories, but Frederick balked. Instead, he wrote to the emperor requesting that Luther's case either be dropped or sent to Germany for a hearing before judges. On December 18, 1518, Frederick wrote a letter to Catejan informing him that he would only send Luther to Rome after he had been convicted of heresy. He urged that Luther be given an opportunity to debate his interpretation of Scripture and submit it to a university for decision. "He should be shown in what respect he is a heretic and not condemned in advance," wrote Frederick. Frederick's views no doubt reflected those of most Germans. One writer of the period reported that he polled people in inns around the territory and found that three out of every four persons he talked to supported Luther.

In Rome, meanwhile, a papal bull (*Cum Postquam*) had been prepared clarifying the Church's position on indulgences. Although the decretal ended some of the worst abuses, it affirmed that the Pope had complete power to absolve temporal punishment through indulgences.

In Germany, Luther's arguments were the talk of the nation. The University of Wittenberg had become a predominantly Lutheran institution while a rival university, the University of Leipzig, had emerged as the champion of traditional Catholic positions. A debate was proposed. Luther would come to Leipzig and defend his views against a prominent professor named John Eck. Despite the protests from some church men appalled at the notion of giving the heretic such a stage, the debate went forward in July 1519. For four sessions over eighteen days, the two intellectual powerhouses argued over free will, Biblical support for indulgences, and the primacy of Rome. In the end, there was no clear winner and only one of the two judging universities (Paris and Erfurt) reported its judgment.

The fame and influence of Luther continued to spread. Between the Leipzig debates and the summer of 1520, Luther wrote and published a series of tracts that are considered his primary works: *The Sermon on Good Works*, *The Papacy in Rome*, *The Babylonian Captivity*, and *The Freedom of the Christian Man*. *The Babylonian Captivity* was an especially controversial book, questioning all but two of the seven sacraments of the Catholic Church.

Rome, however, had not forgotten about Martin Luther. On June 15, 1520, Pope Leo X, in the papal bull *Exsurge Domine*, warned Luther that he will be excommunicated unless he recanted 41 sentences included in his *Ninety-Five Theses* within the next sixty days. The bull opened with a paragraph that compared Luther to a wild boar:

"Arise, O Lord, and judge your own cause. Remember your reproaches to those who are filled with foolishness all through the day. Listen to our prayers, for foxes have arisen seeking to destroy the vineyard whose winepress you alone have trod. When you were about to ascend to your Father, you committed the care, rule, and administration of the vineyard, an image of the triumphant church, to Peter, as the head and your vicar and his successors. The wild boar from the forest seeks to destroy it and every wild beast feeds upon it."

Exsurge Domine ended with a plea and an injunction:

"Therefore let Martin himself and all those adhering to him, and those who shelter and support him, through the merciful heart of our God and the sprinkling of the blood of our Lord Jesus Christ by which and through whom the redemption of the human race and the upbuilding of holy mother Church was accomplished, know that from our heart we exhort and beseech that he cease to disturb the peace, unity, and truth of the Church for which the Saviour prayed so earnestly to the Father. Let him abstain from his pernicious errors that he may come back to us. We enjoin, however, on Martin that in the meantime he cease from all preaching or the office of preacher."

With the papal bull executed and plans for its distribution in the works, Luther's books were burned in Rome's Piazza Navona. In the meantime, Luther had drafted an appeal of his case and sent it to the new emperor of the Holy Roman Empire, Charles V. Often called 'An Appeal to Caesar', Luther's document asked the emperor to allow his guilt or innocence on the heresy charge to be determined after a hearing by non-ecclesiastical officials. Luther boldly asserted in his August appeal that church officials should be answerable to the state:

"For three years I have sought peace in vain. I have now but one recourse. I appeal to Caesar. I have no desire to be defended if I am found to be impious or heretical. One thing I ask, that neither truth nor error be condemned unheard and unrefuted."

It took three months for the papal bull to reach Luther in Wittenberg. The day after receiving a copy of the Pope's bull, Luther wrote to a friend, "This bull condemns Christ himself" and that he was now certain the Pope is the Antichrist. Luther, thoroughly aroused, unleashed a defence of his assertions that received condemnation in the papal bull in his *Against the Execrable Bull of the Antichrist*. The tone of his tract was defiant:

"It is better that I should die a thousand times than that I should retract one syllable of the condemned articles. And as they excommunicated me for the sacrilege of heresy, so I excommunicate them in the name of the sacred truth of God. Christ will judge whose excommunication will stand."

On December 10, 1520, Martin Luther and some of his university supporters gathered at Wittenberg's Elster gate where various theological works and documents from Rome were placed in a pile and lit on fire. Luther himself tossed the papal bull into blaze. "Since they have burned my books, I burn theirs," he said.

With Luther in obvious defiance of his demand for recantation, Pope Leo excommunicated Luther on January 3, 1521. Managing the Luther case for Pope Leo was the papal nuncio, Aleander. In Aleander's view, secular tribunals had no role to play. Luther had been found guilty of heresy, condemned by the Church, and the only job of secular authorities should be to carry out the Church's decision. "The only competent judge is the Pope," Aleander wrote.

When Luther's Appeal to Caesar reached Emperor Charles V, he tore it up and trampled on it. Within a month, however, a more composed Charles V, concerned with the reaction of the German people if Luther were to be condemned without a hearing, reconsidered his decision. On March 11, 1521, the emperor sent to Luther an invitation to come to the Diet meeting at Worms to answer with regard to his books and his teaching. The emperor's mandate promised safe-conduct if he would arrive in Worms within twenty-one days. "You have neither violence nor snares to fear," the letter said.

Luther decided to go. In a letter to Frederick the Wise, Luther explained his thinking: "I will go even if I am too sick to stand on my feet. If Caesar calls me, God calls me. If violence is used, as well it may be, I commend my cause to God."

Luther Before the Diet

Although describing himself as "physically fearful and trembling," Luther and a small band of supporters entered Worms on the early evening of April 16 in a two-wheeled cart. A crowd of two thousand people helped escort Luther to his lodging.

A third-person account, almost certainly written by Luther himself, describes the scene the next day, when Luther was first to be questioned:

At four in the afternoon, the imperial chamberlain, and the herald who had accompanied him from Wittenberg, came to him at his inn, The Court of Germany, and conducted him to the town hall, along bye-ways, in order to avoid the crowds which had assembled in the leading streets. Notwithstanding this precaution, there were numbers collected at the gates of the town hall, and who essayed to enter with him, but the guards kept them back. Many persons had got upon the roofs of houses to see Dr. Martin. As he proceeded to tip the kail, several noblemen successively addressed to him words of encouragement. "Be bold," said they, "and fear not those who can kill the body, but are powerless against the soul."

The Archbishop of Trier, John Eck (not the Eck of the Leipzig debate), opened the hearing by pointing to a large pile of Luther's books and asking him whether the books were his and whether he would retract the doctrines espoused in them. "I think the books are mine," Luther replied. When the titles of the books were read, Luther answered more certainly: "Yes, the books are mine." When asked, "Will you retract the doctrines herein?" Luther answered cautiously saying it would be rash and dangerous to reply to such a question until he had meditated thereupon in silence and retreat, least he incur the anger of their Lord. While expressing surprise that a professor of theology couldn't immediately answer his question, Eck granted Luther's request to think things over. He told Luther to come back the next day at the same time with his answer.

The next day at six o'clock, Luther entered a larger hall that was filled to overflowing. Eck demanded, "Explain yourself now. Will you defend all your writings, or disavow some of them?"

Luther saw an opportunity to give a speech, rather than a "yes" or "no" answer, and he took it. He replied by drawing distinctions between his various writings: "I entreat your majesty and the states of the empire to consider that my writings do not all treat of the same matter. Some of them are perceptive, destined for the edification of the faithful, for the advancement of piety, for the amelioration of manners; yet the bull, while admitting the innocence and advantage of such treatises, condemns these equally with the rest. If I were to disavow them, what practically should I be doing? Proscribing a mode of instruction which every Christian sanctions, and thus putting myself in opposition to the universal voice of the faithful."

Luther then described a second class of writings, "Those in which I attack the papacy and the belief of the papists, as monstrosities, involving the ruin of sound doctrine and of men's souls." He brashly asserted that the Pope's decretals have thrown utter disorder into Christianity, had surprised, imprisoned, and tortured the faith of the faithful...contrary to the gospel. "If he were to retract these writings," Luther said, "he would lend additional strength and audacity to the

Roman tyranny and open the floodgates to the torrent of impiety, making for it a breach by which it would rush in and overwhelm the Christian world."

Finally, Luther said that there was a third class of works in which he had attacked his theological adversaries. For these writings, Luther offered a small apology: "I have no hesitation in admitting that in these I have shown greater violence than befitted a man of my calling; I do not set up for a saint, I do not say that my conduct has been above reproach." Nonetheless, Luther refused to disavow these writings as well because to do so would allow Rome would make use of the disavowal, to extend her kingdom and oppress men's souls.

Luther would not back down. Only if he could be convinced of his errors on the basis of Scripture might he offer a retraction and throw his books into the fire with his own hand. He warned those judging him to not condemn the Divine Word lest God send down upon them a deluge of ills, and the reign of their noble young emperor, upon whom, next to God, repose all their hopes, be speedily and sorely troubled. He ended his speech by entreating the emperor and the lordships to not let his enemies to indulge their hatred against him under the emperor's sanction."

Eck found Luther's answer evasive. He asked again, "Martin, answer candidly and without horns. Do you or do you not repudiate your books and the errors which they contain?"

Luther replied, "'Since then your imperial majesty and your lordships demand a simple answer, I will give you one without teeth and without horns. Unless I am convicted of error by the testimony of Scripture or by manifest evidence, I cannot and will not retract, for we must never act contrary to our conscience. Here I stand. God help me! Amen!"

After, as requested, repeating his answer in Latin (he had spoken in German), a sweating and tired Luther threw up his arms in victory and left the hall to a chorus of hisses from the Spaniards present. Frederick the Wise offered an appraisal of Luther's performance: "Dr. Martin spoke wonderfully before the emperor, the princes, and the estates, but too boldly." Arriving back in his lodging after his two-hour hearing, Luther downed in one gulp a can of Eimbeck beer that had been left for him there by a friend.

Charles V told a group of electors after the hearing that he was ready to proceed against Luther as "a notorious heretic." Most of the electors were in agreement with the emperor, but there were the German peasants to worry about. The peasants were on the verge of a revolt and condemnation of Luther, who they saw as a champion, might push them into open conflict. A committee was selected to meet with Luther and to try to seek at least a partial revocation. The committee's efforts failed. Luther would not compromise on his principles.

On May 6, a final draft of the Edict of Worms, prepared by Aleander, was submitted to the Diet. It was finally signed by the emperor on May 26. The Edict called Luther a "reviver of the old and condemned heresies" and an "inventor of new ones." It called for the burning of his books and for confiscation of his property. It cut him off from the church, called for his arrest, and forbid anyone from harbouring or sustaining him. Finally, it warned that anyone who dares to directly or indirectly oppose the decree will be guilty of the crime of *lese majeste* and will incur their grave indignation as well as each of the punishments mentioned.

By the time the Edict of Worms was announced, Martin Luther was a month gone from Worms. He was, in fact, at Wartburg Castle where he had been hustled on horseback by a gang of "abductors" as part of a staged kidnapping on his route back to Wittenberg. Frederick the Wise had decided to hide him.

The Aftermath

In Wartburg Castle, where Luther occupied himself with translating the Bible into German, he bravely accepted the invitation of Wittenberg's town council to come home. Within days of his return, the exile was – in the defiance of the Pope, the emperor, and the elector – back in the pulpit, beginning a series of important lectures ("the Invocavit Sermons") on core Christian values.

Much of the remainder of Luther's career was devoted to building the liturgy, patterns, and institutions for a new Church, one based on his interpretation of Scripture and his guiding principle of salvation through faith and the grace of God. He also worked tirelessly on his complete translation of the Bible into German.

In 1525, Luther married Katherine von Bora, a nun fifteen years younger than him, whom he had helped escape from a convent. The couple had six children.

The period of 1524-25 is a tumultuous one in Germany, with the outbreak of the Peasants' War, a revolt by the have-nots of Germany against the state and the upper classes. Luther was a hero to many of those in the rebellion because he had publicly sided with the peasants on many of their grievances. When, however, the peasants committed atrocities in his name, Luther called for them to obey authorities and wrote a tract in which he condemned the violence at the devil's work.

In the late 1520s, most of northern Germany became Lutheran, as well as several major cities in other parts of Germany. Meanwhile, the popularity of Luther and his ideas within his home region convinced secular authorities that enforcement of the Edict of Worms is no longer a wise option. In August 1526, the Diet of Speyer reaffirmed the Edict of Worms only for Catholic territories and allowed Lutheranism to be tolerated in regions where it could not be effectively suppressed.

Lutheranism continued its spread and became the dominant faith in Scandinavia and other parts of northern Europe. Much later, of course, it gained an extensive following in the United States. Just as significantly, the Reformation planted the seeds for the growth of other varieties of Protestantism.

Religious wars occupied Europe for a century, finally ending in 1648 with the Peace of Westphalia. With that, the principle of national sovereignty began to dominate both the theory and practice of international relations. Because of Luther, and the events he set in motion, no higher authority stood above nations and only the ceaseless exercise of power kept contending national interests in check. We had come into the modern world.

Martin Luther died at age 62 on February 18, 1546 in Eisleben. He was buried beneath the pulpit in the Castle Church in Wittenberg.

Martin Luther

Born: Nov. 10, 1483, Eisleben, Saxony

Died: Feb. 18, 1546, Eisleben

German priest who sparked the Reformation.

The son of a miner, he studied philosophy and law before entering an Augustinian monastery in 1505. He was ordained two years later and continued his theological studies at the University of Wittenberg, where he became a professor of biblical studies. He was shocked by the corruption of the clergy on a trip to Rome in 1510 and was later troubled by doubts centring on fear of divine retributive justice. His spiritual crisis was resolved when he hit on the idea of justification by faith, the doctrine that salvation is granted as a gift through God's grace. He urged reform of the Roman Catholic church, protesting the sale of indulgences and other abuses, and in 1517 he distributed to the archbishop of Mainz and several friends his *Ninety-Five Theses* (according to legend, Luther nailed the theses to the door of the castle church in Wittenberg); the theses questioned Roman Catholic teaching and called for reform. In 1521, he was excommunicated by Pope Leo IX and declared an outlaw at the Diet of Worms. Under the protection of the elector of Saxony, Luther took refuge in Wartburg. There he translated the Bible into German; his superbly vigorous translation has long been regarded as the greatest landmark in the history of the German language. He later returned to Wittenberg, and in 1525 he married the former nun Katherina von Bora, with whom he raised six children. Though his preaching was the principal spark that set off the Peasants' War (1524–25), his vehement denunciation of the peasants contributed to their defeat. His break with Rome led to the founding of the Lutheran Church; the Lutheran confession of faith or, Augsburg Confession, was produced with Luther's sanction by Philipp Melanchthon in 1530. Luther's writings included hymns, a liturgy, and many theological works.

8. The Trial of Galileo

In the 1633 trial of Galileo Galilei, two worlds come into cosmic conflict. Galileo's world of science and humanism collides with the world of Scholasticism and absolutism that held power in the Catholic Church. The result is a tragedy that marks both the end of Galileo's liberty and the end of the Italian Renaissance.

Galileo Galilei was born in 1564, the same year Shakespeare was born and Michelangelo died. From an early age, Galileo showed his scientific skills. At the age nineteen, he discovered the isochronism of the pendulum. By the age twenty-two, he had invented the hydrostatic balance. By twenty-five, Galileo assumed his first lectureship at the University of Pisa. Within a few more years, Galileo earned a reputation throughout Europe as a scientist and superb lecturer. Eventually, he was recognised as the father of experimental physics. Galileo's motto might have been "follow knowledge wherever it leads us."

At the University of Padua, where Galileo accepted a position after three years in Pisa, he began to develop a strong interest in Copernican theory. In 1543, Nicolaus Copernicus published *Revolutions of the Celestial Orbs*, a treatise that put forth his revolutionary idea that the Sun was at the centre of the universe and that the Earth – rotating on an axis – orbited around the sun once a year. Copernicus' theory was a challenge to the accepted notion contained in the natural philosophy of Aristotle, the astronomy of Ptolemy and the teachings of the Church that the sun and all the stars revolved around a stationary Earth. In the half-century since its publication, however, Copernicus' theory met mostly with skepticism. Skeptics countered with the "common sense" notion that the earth they stood on appeared not to move at all – much less at the speed required to fully rotate every twenty-four hours while spinning around the sun.

Sometime in the mid-1590s, Galileo concluded that Copernicus got it right. He admitted as much in a 1597 letter to Johannes Kepler, a

German mathematician who had written about planetary systems: "Like you, I accepted the Copernican position several years ago and discovered from thence the cause of many natural effects which are

doubtless inexplicable by the current theories." Galileo, however, continued to keep his thoughts to a few trusted friends, as he explained to Kepler: "I have not dared until now to bring my reasons and refutations into the open, being warned by the fortunes of Copernicus himself, our master, who procured for himself immortal fame among a few but stepped down among the great crowd."

Galileo's discovery of the telescope in 1609 enabled him to confirm his beliefs in the Copernican system and emboldened him to make public arguments in its favour. Through a telescope set in his garden behind his house, Galileo saw the Milky Way, the valleys and mountains of the moon, and especially relevant to his thinking about the Copernican system four moons orbiting around Jupiter like a miniature planetary system. Galileo, a good Catholic, offered infinite thanks to God for being so kind as to make him alone the first observer of marvels kept hidden in obscurity for all previous centuries. Galileo began talking about his observations at dinner parties and in public debates in Florence, where he has taken up a new post.

Galileo expected the telescope to quickly make believers in the Copernican system out of all educated persons, but he was disappointed. He expressed his discouragement in a 1610 letter to Kepler: "My dear Kepler, what would you say of the learned here, who replete with the pertinacity of the asp, have steadfastly refused to cast a glance through the telescope? What shall we make of this? Shall we laugh, or shall we cry?" It became clear that the Copernican theory had its enemies.

Galileo's first instinct was turn to acquiring more knowledge for those few open minds he was able to reach – disciples such as monk Benedetto Castelli. Galileo wrote to Castelli: "In order to convince those obdurate men, who are out for the vain approval of the stupid vulgar, it would not be enough even if the stars came down on earth to bring witness about themselves. Let us be concerned only with gaining knowledge for ourselves, and let us find therein our consolation."

Soon, however, Galileo who was flamboyant by nature decided that Copernicus was worth a fight. He decided to address his arguments to the enlightened public at large, rather than the hidebound academics. He saw more hope for gaining support among businessmen, gentlemen, princes, and Jesuit astronomers than among the vested apologists of universities. He seemed compelled to act as a consultant in natural philosophy to all who would listen. He wrote in tracts, pamphlets, letters, and dialogues not in the turgid, polysyllabic manner of a university pedant, but simply and directly.

The Admonition and False Injunction of 1616

In 1613, just as Galileo published his *Letters on the Solar Spots*, an openly Copernican writing, the first attack came from a Dominican friar and professor of ecclesiastical history in Florence, Father Lorini. Preaching on All Soul's Day, Lorini said that Copernican doctrine violated Scripture, which clearly places Earth, and not the Sun at the centre of the universe. What, if Copernicus were right, would be the sense of Joshua 10:13 which says, "So the sun stood still in the midst of heaven" or Isaiah 40:22 that speaks of the heaven stretched out as a curtain above the circle of the earth? Pressured later to apologise for his attack, Lorini later said that he said a couple of words to the effect that the doctrine of Ipernicus (sic), or whatever his name is, was against Holy Scripture.

Galileo responded to criticism of his Copernican views in a December 1613 *Letter to Castelli*. In his letter, Galileo argued that the Scripture although truth itself must be understood sometimes in a figurative sense. A reference, for example, to "the hand of God" is not meant to be interpreted as referring to a five-fingered appendage, but rather to His presence in human lives. Given that the Bible should not be interpreted literally in every case, Galileo contended, it is senseless to see it as supporting one view of the physical universe over another. "Who," Galileo asked, "would dare assert that we know all there is to be known?"

Galileo hoped that his *Letter to Castelli* might foster a reconciliation of faith and science, but it only served to increase the heat. His enemies accused him of attacking Scripture and meddling in theological affairs. One among them, Father Lorini, raised the stakes for the battle when, on February 7, 1615, he sent to the Roman Inquisition a modified copy of Galileo's *Letter to Castelli*. He attached his own comments to his submission:

"All our Fathers of this devout convent of St. Mark are of opinion that the letter contains many propositions which appear to be suspicious or presumptuous, as when it asserts that the language of Holy Scripture does not mean what it seems to mean; that in discussions about natural phenomena the last and lowest place ought to be given the authority of the sacred text; that its commentators have very often erred in their interpretation; that the Holy Scriptures should not be mixed up with anything except matters of religion. When, I say, I became aware of all of this, I made up my mind to acquaint your Lordship with the state of affairs, that you in your holy zeal for the Faith may, in conjunction with your illustrious colleagues, provide such remedies as may appear advisable. I, who hold that those who call themselves Galileists are orderly men and good Christians all, but a little overwise and conceited in their opinions, declare that I am actuated by nothing in this business but zeal for the sacred cause."

In fact, Lorini's letter appears more charitable than he in fact was. He would stop at almost nothing to destroy the "Galileists," as is shown from his alteration in certain key places of the text of Galileo's Letter to Castelli. For example, where Galileo had written: "There are in Scripture words *which, taken in the strict literal meaning, look as if they differed from the truth*." Lorini substituted: "*Which are false in their literal meaning*." However unscrupulous his methods, Lorini's denunciation succeeded in setting the machinery of the Catholic Church in motion.

Lorini had allies, such as Father Tommaso Caccini. Caccini travelled to Rome to appear before the Holy Office and expose, as he saw it, "the errors of Galileo." Called for examination on March 20, Caccini said that Florence was full of "Galileists" publicly declaring God to be an accident and doubting miracles. Caccini placed full blame for the sorry state of affairs on Galileo. Asked the basis for his report, Caccini credited Lorini and a Father Ximenes. Overall, the condemnation was hardly convincing. Giorgio de Santillana, author of *The Crime of Galileo*, wrote of Caccini's testimony: "The whole deposition is such an interminable mass of twists and innuendoes and double talk that a summary does no justice to it."

Matteo Caccini, Tommaso's brother, fumed when he learned of his brother's denunciation of Galileo. He described his brother as "lighter than a leaf and emptier than a pumpkin." In an April letter he wrote of his Tommaso's action: "As to F. T., I am so angry that I could not be more, but I don't care to discuss it. He opened up with me in private the other day, and he revealed such dreadful plans that I could scarcely control myself. In any event, I wash my hands of him forever and ever."

Aware of the move against him, Galileo wrote to a friend, Monsignor Dini, asking that his letters be forwarded to the influential Cardinal Bellarmine, the Church's chief theologian, Pope Paul V. Unfortunately for Galileo, the seventy-four-year old Cardinal Bellarmine was no friend of novelties (although, unlike some of Galileo's other detractors, he had at least looked through a telescope and given – in 1611 – an audience to Galileo). In his innate conservatism, he saw the Copernican universe as threatening to the social order. To Bellarmine and much of the Church's upper echelon, the science of the matter was beyond their understanding and in many cases their interest. They cared about administration and preserving the power of the papal superstate more than they did getting astronomical facts right.

Bellarmine stated his views on the Galileo controversy in an April 12, 1615 letter to Father Foscarini, a highly-respected monk from Naples. He indicated that Galileo could speak about the Copernican model hypothetically, and not absolutely. Bellarmine wrote that to affirm that the Sun, in its very truth, is at the centre of the universe is a very dangerous attitude and one calculated not only to arouse all Scholastic philosophers and theologians but also to injure their faith by contradicting the Scriptures.

With nineteen centuries of organised thought piling up to smother him, Galileo pleaded in a powerful summary of thoughts on Scriptural interpretation and the evidence concerning the nature of the universe – his case in his *Letter to the Grand Duchess*. He asked that his idea not be condemned without understanding it, without hearing it, without even having seen it. Galileo's eloquent *Letter* was forwarded to Rome where, in the words of one historian, "It sank out of sight as softly as a penny in a snowbank."

When depositions in the Galileo matter concluded, the Commissary-General forwarded two propositions of Galileo to eleven theologians (called "Qualifiers") for their evaluation: (1) The Sun is the centre of the world and immovable of local motion, and (2) The Earth is not the centre of the world, nor immovable, but moves according to the whole of itself, also with a diurnal motion. Four days later, on February 23, 1616, the Qualifiers unanimously declared both propositions to be foolish and absurd and formally heretical. Less than two weeks later, Pope Paul V described by the Florentine ambassador as "so averse to anything intellectual that everyone has to play dense and ignorant to gain his favour" – endorsed the theologian's conclusions. The Pope, according to the Inquisition file directed the Lord Cardinal Bellarmine to summon before him the said Galileo and admonish him to abandon the said opinion; and, in the case of his refusal to obey, the Commissary of the Holy Office is to enjoin him...to abstain altogether from teaching or defending this opinion and even from discussing it.

Summoned before Bellarmine on February 25, 1616 and admonished, Galileo, according to a witness, Cardinal Oregius, remained silent with all his science and thus showed that no less praiseworthy than his mind was his pious disposition. Oregius' account, and Galileo's own writings, indicate that Galileo did not "refuse to obey" the Church's admonition. It is assumed, therefore, that Galileo was not formally enjoined. Yet, surprisingly, in the Inquisition file there appeared the following entry:

At the palace, the usual residence of Lord Cardinal Bellarmine, the said Galileo, having been summoned and being present before the said Lord Cardinal, was...warned of the error of the aforesaid opinion and admonished to abandon it; and immediately thereafter...the said Galileo was by the said Commissary *commanded and enjoined*, in the name of His Holiness, the Pope and the whole Congregation of the Holy Office, to relinquish altogether the said opinion that the Sun is the centre of the world and immovable and that the Earth moves; nor further to hold, teach, or defend it in anyway whatsoever, verbally or in writing; otherwise proceedings would be taken against him by the Holy Office; which injunction the said Galileo acquiesced in and promised to obey.

Many things about the entry are suspicious. It appears in the Inquisition file where one would expect the actual Bellarmine injunction (if it existed) to appear. Moreover, the entry appears on the same page as the entry for the previous day and every other report, legal act, and entry in the entire file begins at the top of a new page. It is widely believed by historians that the reported injunction of Galileo was "a false injunction": the injunction never happened, but a false report was maliciously planted in the file by one of Galileo's enemies. Seventeen years later, Galileo would stand before the Inquisition charged with violating an injunction that was, in all likelihood, never issued against him.

The Trial of 1633

Galileo's admonition stopped the Copernican movement dead in its tracks. For Galileo, his admonition marked the beginning of a period of silence. He busied himself with such tasks as using tables of the moons of Jupiter to develop a chronometer for measuring longitude at sea. He endured his rheumatism, enjoyed the attention of his daughter, Maria Celeste, and adjusted to a world which elevated mindless conformism over scientific understanding.

In 1623, Galileo received some hopeful news: Cardinal Maffeo Barberini had been elected Pope. Unlike the dull and mean-tempered

Pope Paul V, the new Pope Urban VIII held a generally positive view of the arts and science. Writing from Rome, the Pope's private secretary, Secretary of the Briefs Ciampoli, urged Galileo to resume publication of his ideas: "If you would resolve to commit to print those ideas that you still have in mind, I am quite certain that they would be most acceptable to His Holiness, who never ceases from admiring your eminence and preserves intact his attachment for you. You should not deprive the world of your productions."

In the early years of his reign, Pope Urban VIII held long audiences with Galileo. Encouraged by a Pope who seemed open to renewed debate on the merits of the Copernican system (so long as the arguments fell short of purporting to be a definite refutation of the Earth-centred universe), Galileo began work on a book that would eventually prove his undoing, *Dialogue Concerning the Two Chief World Systems.*

On December 24, 1629, Galileo told friends in Rome that he had completed work on his 500-page *Dialogue.* The *Dialogue* has been described as "the story of the mind of Galileo." The book reveals Galileo as physicist and astronomer, sophisticate and sophist, polemicist and polished writer. Unlike the works of Copernicus and Kepler, Galileo's *Dialogue* was a book for the educated public, not specialists. Although using the form of a debate among three Italian gentlemen, Galileo marshalled a variety of arguments to lead his readers to one inexorable conclusion: Copernicus was right. The character Salviati, a person of "sublime intellect," clearly speaks for Galileo in arguing for a Sun-centred system. Sagredo is a Venetian nobleman, open-minded and hesitant to draw conclusions and also a good listener. Simplico is the straw man of the debate, a stubborn, literal-minded defender of the Earth-centred universe.

Early news from Rome gave Galileo reason for optimism that his book would soon be published. The Vatican's chief licenser, Niccolo Riccardi, reportedly promised his help and said that theological difficulties could be overcome. When Galileo arrived in Rome in May 1630, he wrote: "His Holiness has begun to treat of my affairs in a spirit which allows me to hope for a favourable result." Urban VIII reiterated his previously stated view that if the book treated the contending views hypothetically and not absolutely, the book could be published.

Reading the book for the first time, chief licenser Riccardi came to see the book as less hypothetical and therefore more problematic than he expected it to be. Riccardi demanded that the Preface and conclusion to be revised to become more consistent with the Pope's position. In August 1630, in the midst of his required revising, Galileo received a letter from his friend Benedetto Castelli in Rome urging him, for "weighty reasons" which he "not wish to commit to paper," to print the *Dialogue* in Florence as soon as possible. Galileo's Jesuit opponents in Rome were aiming to block publication.

Riccardi seemed paralysed with indecision. Caught between two powerful forces, he did nothing as Galileo fretted that his great work might never see the light of day. "The months and the years pass," Galileo complained, "my life wastes away, and my work is condemned to rot."

Finally, reluctantly ("dragged by the hair," according to one account), Riccardi gave the green light. The first copy of Galileo's *Dialogue Concerning the Two Chief World Systems* came off the press in February 1632. The book, which quickly sold out, soon became the talk of the literary public.

By late summer, Galileo's hopes turned to fears when he learned that orders had come from Rome to suspend publication of his book. On September 5, the full scope of Galileo's problems became clearer when Pope Urban told Francesco Niccolini, who had come to the Vatican to protest the suspension decision, "Your Galileo has ventured to meddle in things that he ought not and with the most grave and dangerous subjects that can be stirred up these days." Jesuit enemies of Galileo had convinced the Pope that the *Dialogue* was nothing but a thinly-veiled brief for the Copernican model. The Pope complained that Galileo and Ciampoli deceived him, assuring him that the book would comply with papal instructions and then circumventing them. The Pope seemed especially embittered by Galileo's decision to put the Pope's own argument concerning the tides into the mouth of the simple-minded Simplico – an attempt, as he saw it, to ridicule him.

The Pope swung the machinery of the Church into motion. He appointed a special commission to investigate the Galileo matter. Riccardi, the chief licenser, was severely lectured. Ciampoli was exiled to obscure posts, never to return to Rome.

Galileo, too, became angry. His noble goal of spreading scientific awareness to the public was being frustrated by a narrow-minded bureaucracy intent on preserving its own power. He believed he had done no wrong. He had been authorised to write about Copernicanism, had followed the required form, revised his work to meet censors' objections, and obtained a license. What more could authorities expect? How could the law reach him when he had acted with such care?

The water in which Galileo found himself soon became even deeper. The special commission's report to the Pope outlined a series of indictments against Galileo. On September 15, the Pope turned the matter over to the Inquisition. Eight days later, the General Congregation declared which came as a shock to Galileo – that he had violated the 1616 (so-called) injunction against teaching, holding, or writing about Copernican theory.

On October 1, 1632, the Inquisitor of Florence showed up at Galileo's house with summons to present himself to the Holy Office in Rome within a month. In despair, Galileo expressed regret for involving himself with the Copernican cause: "I curse the time devoted to these studies in which I strove and hoped to move away somewhat from the beaten path. I repent having given the world a portion of my writings; I feel inclined to consign what is left to the flames and thus placate at last the inextinguishable hatred of my enemies." The fire left his belly. He declined urgings to escape to the Venetian territory and instead asked that proceedings against him be moved to Florence. His request was denied. The Pope insisted that the old man, weak and ill though he was, make the two-hundred mile wintertime journey to Rome.

On February 13, 1633, Galileo completed his twenty-three day trip to Rome and took up lodging in the Florentine embassy. It was not a good time. The Grand Duke reported that Galileo for two nights continuously cried and moaned in sciatic pain; and for his advancing age and sorrow. His only consolation during his stay at the embassy seemed to be that soon he would finally have a chance to defend his science and theology.

On April 8, Niccolini informed Galileo that he would stand trial before ten cardinals. A more difficult chore for Niccolini was to break the news to him that the merits of his case, as a practical matter had been decided already; all he could do was submit.

Four days later, Galileo officially surrendered to the Holy Office and faced Father Firenzuola, the Commissary-General of the Inquisition, and his assistants. Firenzuola informed Galileo that for the duration of the proceedings against him he would be imprisoned in the Inquisition building. After putting Galileo under oath, the Commissary deposed Galileo concerning meetings he held with Cardinal Bellarmine and other church officials in 1616. Galileo seemed to have trouble remembering who might have been present with Bellarmine on that fateful February day seventeen years earlier, as well as exactly what restrictions if any had been placed upon him. Firenzuola told Galileo that he had been commanded to neither hold, defend, nor teach that (the Copernican) opinion in any way whatsoever. Galileo quibbled with the language suggesting, "I do not remember...the clause in any way whatsoever", but accepted most of what the Commissary said. After a series of questions concerning the licensing of the *Dialogue*, Galileo signed his deposition in a shaking hand.

Three counsellors to the Inquisition, driven especially by Galileo-hating Melchior Inchofer, prepared a seven-page evaluation of the *Dialogue*. The report concluded that in the book Galileo taught, defended, and showed that he held Copernican theory, and that while claiming to discuss world models hypothetically he gave the Copernican model "a physical reality."

Weeks past as internal debates raged over what the Inquisitors should do with their old scientist. Finally, Cardinal Francesco Barberini, a moderating influence on the panel of ten judges deciding Galileo's fate, persuaded the Commissary to meet Galileo and convince him to admit error in return for a more lenient sentence. In a letter written by the Commissary (and not discovered until 1833), Firenzuola described his April 27 discussion with Galileo: "I entered into discourse with Galileo yesterday afternoon, and after many arguments and rejoinders had passed between us, by God's grace, I attained my object, for I brought him to a full sense of his error, so that he clearly recognised that he had erred and had gone too far in his book."

Some historians have seen Galileo's decision to admit error as a "final self-degradation." Others, including Giorgio de Santillana, have seen it as the only rational move open to him: "He was not a religious visionary being asked to renounce his vision. He was an intelligent man who had taken heavy risks to force an issue and to change a policy for the good of his faith. He had been snubbed; he had nothing to do but pay the price and go home. The scientific truth would take care of itself."

The trial by the Congregation moved to its conclusion. Several of the ten cardinals apparently pushed for Galileo's incarceration in prison, while those more supportive of Galileo argued that with changes the *Dialogue* ought to continue to be allowed to circulate. In the end, a majority of the cardinals, rejecting much of the Commissary's agreement with Galileo demanded Galileo even with the threat of torture...abjure in a plenary assembly of the Congregation of the Holy Office...and then be condemned to imprisonment at the pleasure of the Holy Congregation. Moreover, the cardinals declared, the *Dialogue* should to be prohibited.

The grand play ran its course, with the Pope insisting upon a formal sentence, a tough examination of Galileo, public abjuration, and formal prison. Galileo was forced to appear once again for formal questioning about his true feelings concerning the Copernican system. Galileo obliged, so as not to risk being branded a heretic, testifying that – "I held, as I still hold, as most true and indisputable, the opinion of Ptolemy, that is to say, the stability of the Earth and the motion of the Sun." Galileo's renunciation of Copernicanism ended with the words, "I affirm, therefore, on my conscience, that I do not now hold the condemned opinion and have not held it since the decision of authorities... I am here in your hands – do with me what you please."

On the morning of June 22, 1633, Galileo, dressed in the white shirt of penitence, entered the large hall of the Inquisition building. He knelt and listened to his sentence: "Whereas you, Galileo, the son of the late Vincenzo Galilei, Florentine, aged seventy years, were in the year 1615 denounced to this Holy Office for holding as true the false doctrine....." The reading continued for seventeen paragraphs:

"And, so that you will be more cautious in future, and an example for others to abstain from delinquencies of this sort, we order that the book *Dialogue of Galileo Galilei* be prohibited by public edict. We condemn you to formal imprisonment in this Holy Office at our pleasure.

As a salutary penance we impose on you to recite the seven penitential psalms once a week for the next three years. And we reserve to ourselves the power of moderating, commuting, or taking off, the whole or part of the said penalties and penances.

This we say, pronounce, sentence, declare, order and reserve by this or any other better manner or form that we reasonably can or shall think of. So we the undersigned Cardinals pronounce."

Seven of the ten cardinals signed the sentence.

Following the reading of the sentence, Galileo knelt to recite his abjuration.

Desiring to remove from the minds of your Eminences, and of all faithful Christians, this strong suspicion, reasonably conceived against me, with sincere heart and unfeigned faith, I abjure, curse, and detest the aforesaid errors and heresies, and generally every other error and sect whatsoever contrary to the said Holy Church; and I swear that in the future I will never again say or assert, verbally or in writing, anything that might furnish occasion for a similar suspicion regarding me.

I, the said Galileo Galilei, have abjured, sworn, promised, and bound myself as above; and in witness of the truth thereof I have with my own hand subscribed the present document of my abjuration, and recited it word for word at Rome, in the Convent of Minerva, this twenty-second day of June, 1633.

I, Galileo Galilei, have abjured as above with my own hand."

Two days later, Galileo was released to the custody of the Florentine ambassador. Niccolini described his charge as "extremely downcast over his punishment." After six days in the custody of Niccolini, custody of Galileo transferred to Archbishop Piccolomini in Sienna. In late 1633, Galileo received permission to move into his own small farmhouse in Arcetri, where he would grow blind and, in 1642, die.

Galileo

Born: Feb. 15, 1564, Pisa

Died: Jan. 8, 1642, Arcetri, near Florence

Italian mathematician, astronomer, and physicist.

Son of a musician, he studied medicine before turning his attention to mathematics. His invention of the hydrostatic balance (c. 1586) made him famous. In 1589, he published a treatise on the centre of gravity in solids, which won him the post of mathematics lecturer at the University of Pisa. There he disproved the Aristotelian contention that bodies of different weights fall at different speeds; he also proposed the law of uniform acceleration for falling bodies and showed that the path of a thrown object is a parabola. The first to use a telescope to study the skies, he discovered (1609–10) that the surface of the Moon is irregular, that the Milky Way is composed of stars, and that Jupiter has moons. His findings led to his appointment as philosopher and mathematician to the grand duke of Tuscany. During a visit to Rome (1611), he spoke persuasively for the Copernican system, which put him at odds with Aristotelian professors and led to Copernicanism's being declared false and erroneous (1616) by the church. Obtaining permission to write about the Copernican system so long as he discussed it noncommittally, he wrote his *Dialogue Concerning the Two Chief World Systems* (1632). Though considered a masterpiece, it enraged the Jesuits, and Galileo was tried before the Inquisition, found guilty of heresy, and forced to recant. He spent the rest of his life under house arrest, continuing to write and conduct research even after going blind in 1637.

9. The Trial of *Al Capone*

Al Capone, head of the most profitable crime syndicate of the Prohibition Era and mastermind of the notorious 1929 "Valentine's Day Massacre," seemed above the law. In the end, however, Capone would be brought to justice not for murder, extortion, or bootlegging, but for failing to pay his income tax. Credit for his conviction is due less to Elliot Ness and The Untouchables than to the dogged work of Bureau of Revenue investigator Frank Wilson and a clever surprise pulled by a federal judge, James Wilkerson. Al Capone once complained about the bad reputation of his criminal enterprise: "Some call it bootlegging. Some call it racketeering. I call it a business." The lesson of *The People vs. Al Capone* is that a profitable businessman, no matter how he earns his income, *does* have to pay his taxes.

Twenty-year-old Al Capone arrived in Chicago in 1919 to help run Johnny Torrio's bootlegging operation. It was Capone's job to keep the competition in line, and he did so with ruthless efficiency. When Torrio left Chicago in 1925, driven out by a maiming and death threats, Capone took over the bootlegging operation. Operating from his headquarters at the Hawthorne Inn in Cicero (with its bulletproof shutters on every window), Capone dispatched his enforcers. On April 27, 1925, a five-car motorcade carrying Capone's trigger men swept by members of a rival bootlegging gang as they left a bar and opened fire with machine guns. One of the men killed, it turned out, was not a known bootlegger but rather Bill McSwiggin, an assistant state's attorney. Chicagoans were used to reports of gang members killing other gang members, but the murder of a top law enforcement officer was something new and the public looked for a response to the growing violence in their city. Authorities charged Capone with the McSwiggin murder, but the fix was in and, six grand juries and no indictments later, charges were dropped.

By 1926, while still maintaining offices in Cicero, Capone had moved his headquarters to fifty rooms of Chicago's Hotel Metropole. With the city's new mayor, Big Bill Thompson, in his pocket, Capone carried out his illegal bootlegging, racketeering, and gambling businesses with virtual impunity. His enforcers carried officially stamped cards issued by the city that read: "To the Police Department – you will extend the courtesies of this department to the bearer."

When Chicago's winters were to much to bear, Capone headed south to his luxurious Miami estate, surrounded by a ten-foot concrete wall, where he could direct operations poolside or from his thirty-two foot cabin cruiser. By 1928, Capone's syndicate was grossing an estimated $105,000,000 a year. Capone liked to think of himself not as a ruthless criminal, but as a public benefactor. "I've given people light pleasures," he said, "shown them a good time."

Capone chose to view the killing of rival gang members as a necessary evil: "Killing a man in defence of your business is like the law of self-defence, a little broader than the law books look at it." On May 7, 1928, Capone held a banquet to which he invited three former associates, men he knew had joined in a plot to assassinate him, but men who still thought they were on good terms with Capone. Drunk and full, the three men suddenly found themselves surrounded by Capone's men who tied each to a chair. Capone pulled out a baseball bat and with shocking deliberation beat each man to death. The best known of the Capone-ordered killings came on Valentine's Day 1929. While seven member of George "Bugs"

Moran's bootlegging gang waited in a Chicago warehouse, expecting the arrival of a truckload of whiskey, a Cadillac carrying six of Capone's men, four dressed in police uniforms, pulled up in front of the warehouse. The members of the Moran gang fell amidst a hail of bullets from machine guns, bodies strewn against a yellow brick wall. Few doubted who the killers were. "Only Capone kills like that," Moran said.

The Treasury Department Launches an Investigation

Capone in 1929 might have been worth about $30 million, but no income tax return had ever been filed in his name. Two years earlier, in *United States v. Sullivan*, the Supreme Court had ruled that the Fifth Amendment's privilege against self-incrimination did not protect Manley Sullivan, a bootlegger convicted of failing to file a return showing the profits from his illegal businesses. With the *Sullivan* case in mind, President Herbert Hoover instructed Secretary of the Treasury Andrew Mellon, "I want that man Capone in jail." Secretary Mellon summoned Elmer Irey, head of Treasury's Special Intelligence Unit, and told him that his office was charged with the responsibility of putting Capone behind bars. For the day-to-day job of gathering incriminating evidence for Capone's tax evasion case, Irey turned to Frank Wilson, his most aggressive and relentless investigator.

Frank Wilson and his team of five other Treasury investigators set up offices in the Chicago Post Office Building and set about the job of building a case against Capone. Capone made their task difficult by not maintaining a bank account and never signing any cheques or receipts. An extravagant life style could be evidence of substantial unreported income, so investigators examined department store, jewellery store, car dealership, and hotel records for evidence of Capone's expenditures. They uncovered purchases of high-end furniture, custom-made shirts, diamond-studded belt buckles, gold plated dinner service, hotel suites, and a Lincoln limousine. They tracked down telephone bills totaling $39,000 and evidence that he paid thousands to host a luxurious party on the night of the Dempsey-Tunney heavyweight fight. While such unusual extravagance does not in itself prove taxable income, a juror could easily draw such an inference.

While successful in tracking down evidence of expenses, investigators encountered considerable difficulty in finding direct evidence of income. As Frank Wilson recalled years later, "I prowled the crummy streets of Cicero, where a twitch of Al's little finger had the force of an edict, but there was no clue that a dollar from the big gambling places, the horse parlours, the brothels, or the bootleg joints ever reached his coffers." Potential witnesses, when subpoenaed, rarely cooperated. Wilson described most as either hostile to government and ready to give perjured testimony or so full of fear of the Capone organisations that they evaded, lied, or left town.

To convict Capone would require help from inside Capone's illicit operation, but for reasons all too obvious, few on the inside wanted to step forward to help the government make its case. One who did was Eddie O'Hare, owner of the patent for the mechanical rabbit used in greyhound racing. O'Hare ran dog racing tracks for the Capone syndicate in the Chicago area, as well as in Florida and Massachusetts. Years later, just days before Capone's release from prison, O'Hare paid the ultimate price for the leads he provided the government over the course of their two-year investigation. While driving on a Chicago street, he was gunned down by two men in a passing car. His son, Edward O'Hare, was the first naval aviator to win the Congressional Medal of Honour. In 1949, Chicago's new international airport was named in Edward's memory.

The first big break in the investigation came in the summer of 1930 when Wilson stumbled across three bound ledgers seized in a 1926 raid of one of Capone's establishments. The ledger was divided into columns with labels such as "Craps," "21," and "Roulette." Every few pages totals were entered and then divided into smaller amounts among "Town," "Ralph," "Pete," and "A." With the ledger also including a few references to "Al" it wasn't much of a leap to conclude that the ledger recorded the monthly income from a gambling hall that went to Capone and his associates. Building on the ledger evidence, Wilson collected sworn testimony from persons whose participation in a citizen's raid on a Cicero gambling hall had left them convinced beyond any doubt that Capone was the proprietor of the place.

An even more significant potential witness was located by comparing the handwriting in the ledger with that on deposit slips from local banks. Investigators identified the likely author of the ledger as

Leslie Shumway, the same man who signed deposit slips that turned up at a small Cicero bank. Agents tracked Shumway to Florida, where they interrupted a breakfast at his home to offer him a ride down to the Miami Federal Building to talk to agents. Threatened with a not-so-secret subpoena and well aware of what Capone might do to someone about to disclose embarrassing facts to the government, Shumway agreed to talk. In his affidavit, Shumway described the nature of the gambling businesses and stated, "I took orders relating to the business from Mr. Alphonse Capone." Almost immediately after Shumway put his signature on the affidavit, agents took him off to California, where they hoped he could be safely hid until trial.

In April 1930, Capone's tax attorney, Lawrence Mattingly, contacted Treasury and expressed the desire to have his client meet with agents to settle his indebtedness with the government. At the Federal Building in Chicago, Wilson and other agents interviewed Capone. In response to the question, "How long, Mr. Capone, have you enjoyed a large income?", Capone replied, "I never had much of an income." At the end of the interview, Capone grew testy. As he prepared to leave the room after the interview, he inquired, "How's your wife, Wilson?" If their doubt as to whether that was a question or a threat, the doubt was resolved when Capone added, "You be sure to take care of yourself."

On September 30, Mattingly met with Wilson to discuss Capone's tax liability. He took a letter from his coat pocket and threw it over to the agent, saying, "This is the best we can do. Mr. Capone is willing to pay the tax on these figures." The so-called "Mattingly letter" conceded taxable income for the six disputed years ranging from $26,000 in 1924 to $100,000 in 1928 and 1929. Wilson filed the letter away. A year later, the letter became the trial's most contentious piece of evidence.

Wilson, not a person easily intimidated, continued to identify witnesses and amass incriminating evidence. One of the last and most important witnesses to be discovered was Fred Reis, the named payee on numerous large cashier cheques that Treasury assumed found their way into Capone's coffers. Reis decided to talk after having four solitary days to think about it in a cockroach-infested jail in Danville, Illinois. He admitted, first to agents and then in testimony before a

Chicago grand jury, that his boss was Capone, and that the cheques represented Capone's net profits at his Cicero gambling hall.

With Reis's statement, prosecutors decided they had enough evidence to go before a grand jury. (After completing his grand jury testimony, Reis was shipped off to South America for safekeeping until trial.) On March 13, two days before the statute of limitations would have run, the grand jury indicted Al Capone for evading federal income taxes in 1924. Two months later, the grand jury added counts for the years 1925 to 1929.

Over the three months that followed, Capone's attorneys met frequently with U. S. Attorney George E.Q. Johnson to discuss a possible plea bargain. With witnesses to try to keep alive and with thorny legal questions concerning the charges, Johnson was willing to listen, hoping to get a two-and-a-half year sentence out of the negotiations. With an agreement for the two-and-a-half year sentence apparently in place, Al Capone appeared on June 18, 1931 before Federal Judge James H. Wilkerson and entered a plea of guilty. Wilkerson adjourned court until July 30 to consider the plea.

On the day before his expected sentencing, Capone told reporters, "I've been made an issue and I'm not complaining, but why don't they go after all those bankers who took the savings of thousands of poor people and lost them in bank failures?" The next day, Judge Wilkerson surprised nearly everyone. Addressing Capone in his pea-green suit, Wilkerson announced, "The parties to a criminal case may not stipulate as to the judgment to be entered." There would be no plea bargain. There would be a trial. Wilkerson continued, "It is time for somebody to impress upon the defendant that it is utterly impossible to bargain with a Federal Court."

Trial

About two weeks before the scheduled start of the Capone trial, informant Eddie O'Hare notified Wilson that Capone's organisation had a complete list of prospective jurors and was already passing out $1,000 bills, promising political jobs, giving away tickets to prize fights, and using muscle too. Skeptical of O'Hare's claim at first, Wilson quickly came around when O'Hare produced the names and addresses of ten jurors, names 30 to 39 on the jury list. Concerned that thousands of hours of work was about to go down the drain because of a fixed jury, Wilson and U. S. Attorney Johnson related O'Hare's story to Judge Wilkerson in his chambers. Wilkerson told the men that he hadn't yet received his jury list for the Capone trial, but when he did he would call them. When the names on Wilkerson's list turned out to match exactly with the names on O'Hare's list, the judge met once again with Wilson and prosecutors. The judge seemed curiously unconcerned. "Bring your case into court as planned, gentlemen," he told the government's attorneys, "leave the rest to me."

The Trial of Alphonse Capone opened on the morning of October 5, 1931 at the federal courthouse in downtown Chicago. Capone, accompanied by his bodyguard, smiled at jurors as he strolled into court in his mustard-coloured suit. Judge Wilkerson took his seat at the bench and looked out over the packed courtroom. He called the bailiff to the bench. "Judge Edwards has another trial commencing today," he told the bailiff. "Go to his courtroom and bring me his entire panel of jurors; take my entire panel to Judge Edwards."

After a jury of twelve was seated, and after Assistant U. S. Attorney Dwight Green outlined the 23 charges of tax evasion against Capone in the government's opening statement, George Johnson called his first witness. Charles W. Arndt, a tax collector for the United States, told jurors that Al Capone failed to file any tax return at all during the years 1924 to 1929.

The prosecution presented evidence that Capone owned gambling halls and derived substantial profits from those businesses. Chester Bragg testified that when he participated in the citizens' raid on the Hawthorne Smoke Shop, a gambling hall in Cicero, Capone arrived on the scene. As Bragg guarded the front door while other citizens carted out gambling machines and loaded them into trucks, Capone attempted to push his way in. Bragg testified that he asked Capone,

"What the hell, do you think this is a party?" And Capone answered, "I'm the owner of this place." Reverend Henry Hoover, leader of the Cicero raid, also testified. Hoover said that Capone complained to him during the raid, "Why are you fellows always picking on me?" and warned, "This is the last raid you'll ever pull." Leslie Shumway, the cashier at the Hawthorne Smoke Shop, presented the most damning evidence of the day. Shumway described the accounting procedures used at the gambling hall and estimated that the profits for the two years he worked there were over $550,000. When Shumway balked at positively identifying Capone as the owner of the establishment, prosecutors tried a different tack, asking questions whose answers seemed to assume Capone exercised control over the business. Jacob Grossman asked Shumway, "Did you any time after that have any conversation with Al Capone about carrying money over there?" The witness answered, "It was some time later that Al asked me what I would do if I got stuck up, and I told him that I would just let them take it, and he says, 'That is right.'"

On October 8, the courtroom erupted in heated debate when the prosecution sought to introduce the letter of Capone's tax lawyer, Lawrence Mattingly, which expressed his willingness to settle his client's tax liability for the years 1924 to 1929. Defence attorney Albert Fink argued, "A lawyer cannot confess for his client." Surely, Fink noted, Capone never meant to give Mattingly the "authority to make statements that may get him into the penitentiary." The controversy developed with Frank Wilson on the stand, describing the events in his office the previous fall when Mattingly first tossed the letter in his direction with the statement, "This is the best we can do. Mr. Capone is willing to pay the tax on these figures." After argument on the letter's admissibility with the jury, Judge Wilkerson announced his decision – the letter would be admitted to show that the statement was made, but the contents of the letter could not be considered by the jury as proof of the statements made.

A series of prosecution witnesses presented evidence of Capone's lavish lifestyle. Parker Henderson testified that he sold Capone his Palm Island, Florida estate, with the title placed in his wife's name. "I asked Al if he was interested in buying any property and he said he was," Henderson told jurors. "So we made an appointment with him and carried him out and showed him several places. This place on

Palm Island he seemed to like very much. Later he told me that he had decided to take it. He gave me all money to put up the binder." Morrissey Smith, a clerk at Chicago's Metropole Hotel told jurors that Capone purchased the hotel's most expensive suites and hosted expensive parties. Asked in what denominations Capone would pay his bills, Smith replied, "Oh, hundred dollar bills, sometimes five hundred dollar bills." Smith's comment prompted gasps from many of the courtroom's depressed and impoverished spectators. Florida dock-builder H. F. Ryder testified that he saw enough money in Capone's Palm Island estate cupboard.

The final key witness for the prosecution was Fred Reis, cashier of the Cicero gambling house in 1927. Reis placed the hall's profits for 1927 at around $150,000. Reis testified that he saw Capone when he was taking bets in the hall. "Capone came by and said, 'Hello, Reis.' I said, 'Hello, Al.'" Jacob Grossman asked Reis about 43 cashier's cheques, representing the hall's profits, that were purchased from a Cicero bank. Reis testified that he had bought the cheques (made out to "J.C. Dunbar," an alias used by Reis) and turned them over to Bobby Barton. Underneath the signature of J.C. Dunbar on one of the cheques was the signature of Al Capone.

The defence presented its case in a single day. Defence attorneys tried to present Capone as a horse-racing addict who lost as much money as his businesses earned during the years in question. (Gambling losses are only deductible against gambling winnings, so even if the defence testimony was accepted, it would hardly have absolved Capone from his duty to pay taxes on the income from his many businesses.) Bookie Milton Held testified that Capone lost three or four hundred dollars at a time betting on horses, and that he was a consistent loser. Oscar Gutter, another bookie, estimated that Capone lost $60,000 betting with him in 1927. After its parade of six bookies had ended, the defence rested its case, having shown that Capone might have lost $327,000 in six years of betting.

In his summation for the defence, Albert Fink told the jury to stand as a bulwark against an oppressive government that was just using the tax law as a means to stow Al Capone away. He described the government's evidence against his client as chaff and that does not to prove gross income. He urged the jury not to convict Capone merely because he was a bad man: "He may be the worst man who ever lived, but there is not a scintilla of evidence that he willfully attempted to defraud the government out of income tax." Then Fink switched gears and concluded by arguing that far from being a bad man, Capone was open-handed, generous, and the kind of man who never fails a friend. "Capone was not the type of miser or tinhorn or piker who would try to cheat the government out of its due," Fink said. Michael Ahern, summing second for the defence, returned to the theme of an oppressive government bent on using questionable means to put Capone in jail to satisfy the newspapers and the persecutors. "You, gentlemen," he told the jury, "are the last barrier between the defendant and the encroachment and perversion of the government and the law in this case."

Prosecutor Jacob Grossman noted in his summation that Capone described himself as a gambler, a realtor, a cleaner and a presser and a dog race-track owner. He pointed out that the defendant lived like a bejeweled prince and spent thousands of dollars without thinking twice. Samuel Clawson emphasised the incriminating nature of the Mattingly letter, which he said proved that Capone knew he was guilty of tax evasion. He added that even a child could deduce from Capone's lavish lifestyle that he had a huge income. The last lawyer to address the jury was U. S. Attorney George Johnson. Johnson said, "This is a case that future generations will remember. They will remember it because it will establish whether a man can so conduct his affairs that he is above the government and above the law."

At 2:42 p.m. on October 18, the jury left the courtroom to begin its deliberations. They filed back into the courtroom eight hours later with their verdict in hand. When the clerk pronounced the word "guilty" (on the charge of tax evasion for 1925) reporters dashed to phones to report the news. Six days later, Judge Wilkerson imposed a prison sentence of eleven years, the longest term ever handed down for tax evasion. Capone, as he was led in handcuffs to a courtroom elevator, yelled, "I'm not through fighting yet."

Appeals failed. Capone served time in federal penitentiaries in Atlanta and at Alcatraz. In November 1939, after serving less than eight years, he was released while suffering from paresis caused by untreated syphilis. On January 25, 1947, Capone died of a stroke in Palm Island, Florida.

Al Capone

Born: Jan. 17, 1899, Brooklyn, N.Y., U.S.

Died: Jan. 25, 1947, Palm Island, Fla.

U.S. gangster.

Quitting school after the sixth grade, he joined the James Street Boys gang, led by Johnny Torrio. In a youthful fight in a brothel-saloon, he was slashed across the left cheek with a knife or razor, prompting the later nickname "Scarface." In 1919, he joined Torrio in Chicago to help run the giant brothel business there. When Torrio retired (1925), Capone became the city's crime czar, running gambling, prostitution, and bootlegging rackets. He expanded his territory by killing his rivals, most famously in the St. Valentine's Day Massacre, in which members of the Bugs Moran gang were machine-gunned in a garage on Feb. 14, 1929. In 1931, Capone was convicted for income-tax evasion and sentenced to 11 years in prison; eventually he served time in the infamous prison Alcatraz. Suffering from paresis (a late stage of syphilis), he was released in 1939 and later retired to Florida, where he died a powerless recluse.

10. The Trial of *Nelson Mandela*

It's the trial that changed South Africa. In the fall of 1963, Nelson Mandela and ten other leading opponents of South Africa's apartheid regime faced trial for their lives. The charges, what is often called "the Rivonia trial" for the Johannesburg suburb which was the location of the hideout for a militant wing of the African National Congress, were sabotage and conspiracy, and there was little doubt that Mandela and most of the other defendants would be found guilty. Desperate times had dictated desperate measures. Standing in the dock at the Palace of Justice in Pretoria, Mandela announced, "The ideal of a democratic and free society is one for which I am prepared to die."

Rivonia Discovered

Lieutenant van Wyk, his informant were a week into their search for what the informant insisted was the hideaway of the ANC and members of its military wing, Umkhonto we Sizwe. Finally, as the two men travelled yet another road in Johannesburg's northern suburbs, the informant spotted a gabled house that he recognised. Down the next bend in the road, near a weathered sign bearing the name "Rivonia," the informant saw a gate that he said stood a few hundred yards from a farmhouse that was the secret meeting place of the leadership of South Africa's most determined anti-apartheid activists.

The next day, July 11, 1963, fourteen police officers and a police dog piled into a laundry van and entered Lilliesleaf, an estate owned by Arthur Goldreich. The men leaped out as the van stopped in front of the homestead and then quickly surrounded the building. Inside the home, the police found Denis Goldberg. In an thatched-roof outbuilding, police discovered two whites and one Bantu. More significantly, as their search of the room continued, they found a six-page typed document labelled "Operation Mayibuye." When it was over, the raid would yield eight suspects: Goldberg, Rusty Bernstein,

Raymond Mhlaba, Bob Hepple, Govan Mbeki, Arthur Goldreich, Ahmed Kathrada, and ANC leader Walter Sisulu. The police carted away dozens of documents – letters, pamphlets, Communist literature, and maps. They also took a radio transmitter and a duplicating machine. The prosecution's case in the Rivonia trial would, to a large extent, be built around what was found in the Rivonia raid. Authorities announced to the nation the Rivonia raid in exultant tones.

Nelson Mandela Faces New Charges

At the time of the Rivonia raid, Nelson Mandela was lodged in solitary confinement at a Pretoria jail serving a five-year prison term for leaving the country without a passport and inciting a strike.

Mandela played a key role in bringing the ANC to the view that force had to be met with force if black liberation were ever to come to South Africa. After calling for a general strike in May 1960, Mandela had vanished underground. The strike attracted less support than Mandela hoped, and he began telling friends that the days of nonviolent struggle were over. In June 1960, Mandela proposed to the ANC executive the undertaking of an armed effort against the South African government: "The attacks of the the wild beast cannot be averted with only bare hands," he said. The ANC executive initially decided, however, that the time was not ripe to take up arms.

Eventually, Mandela's arguments won over the ANC, which voted to establish a separate and independent military organ, Umkhonto we Sizwe, or "Spear of the Nation". In June 1961, Mandela sent to South African newspapers a letter warning that a new campaign would be launched unless the government agreed to call for a national constitutional convention. Knowing that no such call would be forthcoming, Mandela retreated to the Rivonia hideout to

began planning, with other supporters, a sabotage campaign. The campaign began on December 16, 1961 when Umkhonto we Sizwe saboteurs lit explosives at an electricity sub-station. Dozens of other acts of sabotage followed over the next eighteen months. Indeed, the government would allege the defendants committed 235 separate acts of sabotage. The sabotage included attacks on government posts, machines, and power facilities, as well as deliberate crop burning.

Mandela spent much of the early months of the sabotage campaign at the Rivonia safe house, where he went by the name of David. At Rivonia, Mandela met with other leaders to shape strategy and plan a possible future guerrilla war against the South African government. His goal, he always said, was not to establish a government ruled by blacks, but to move to a multi-racial democracy that would abolish repressive laws that separated African families, restricted their travel, imposed curfews, and denied other basic human rights. In February 1962, Mandela left South Africa to garner support from foreign governments for the goals of the ANC and to receive six months of military training is Addis Ababa, Ethiopia. Acting on a tip, probably from the CIA, South African officials arrested Mandela shortly after his return in October.

In July 1963, Mandela learned of the Rivonia raid when he was summoned to the office of a Pretoria prison and saw ten other men who, with him, sometimes would be called the "Rivonia 11." The men included seven captured at Rivonia, plus two who were previously detained (Andrew Mlangeni and Elias Motsoaledi), and James Kantor, an attorney. All the other men were being held under the new Ninety-Day Detention Law that allowed security officials to hold without charges for ninety days persons suspected of political crimes. During this period, the men were denied the opportunity to consult with lawyers or see their families. Most were held in solitary confinement and some were tortured.

Two other men – Harold Wolpe, lawyer for the ANC and a radical activist, had been arrested in a disguise near the Bechuanaland border as they attempted to flee South Afrca a few days after the Rivonia raid. Arthur Goldreich, a noted painter and the owner of Lilliesleaf Farm in Rivonia, had been picked up in the July 11 raid. Both men had helped identify sabotage targets for Umkhonto we Sizwe. The two men avoided trial by pulling off the most dramatic escape in South African history. They convinced their financially hard-up prison guard to give them their cell keys and play the victim of a simulated assault in exchange for 2000 pounds. Wolpe and Goldreich slipped out of prison and disappeared into the midnight darkness. Eventually, they made their way to a garden cottage in a Johannesburg suburb, where they stayed hidden for a week to let the search for them cool down. Finally, dressed as priests, they travelled overland to Swaziland where they chartered a flight to Bechuanaland. In Bechuanaland, South African agents blew up the plane that was scheduled to take them on to Tanganyika, but persons outside the country arranged for a small plane to fly into a remote airstrip and the two men finally landed in the safe haven of Dar-es-Salaam, Tanganyika.

The defendants first chance to meet with defence attorneys, Bram Fischer, Joel Joffe, George Bizos, and Arthur Chaskalson did not come until October 8, 1963, the night before their trial was scheduled to begin. At the time, neither the lawyers nor the defendants knew what crimes the government would charge. Whatever the charges against them, nine of the defendants agreed that they would enter a joint defence. James Kantor, it was decided, needed his own counsel since he had no connection with the other defendants and was seemingly charged only as a proxy for his brother-in-law and law partner, Harold Wolpe. Bob Hepple had been pushed by authorities to become state's witness in return for immunity from prosecution, and announced to the group that he was uncertain about whether to accept the state's offer. Clearly, Hepple had to find his own lawyer and be left out of future defence strategy sessions.

Trial

The next day at the Palace of Justice in Pretoria, in a segregated courtroom filled on one side with plain-clothed police officers and on the other side with relatives and friends of the accused, prosecutor Percy Yutar called the case of "State versus the National High Command and Others." He then produced an indictment charging the eleven defendants with two counts of sabotage and two counts of conspiracy. The defence, noting that they were just then seeing the indictment for the first time, asked Justice Quartus de Wet for a postponement. De Wet gave the defence three weeks to prepare for trial.

When court reconvened three weeks later, Nelson Mandela led the parade of defendants up a staircase that opened into the centre of the court, where a specially constructed dock had been built. Mandela gave the clenched fist salute to supporters that had become an ANC trademark. Mandela shouted, "Amandla!" (Power), and the crowd responded with the cry, "Ngawethu!" (It shall be ours).

Defence attorney Bram Fischer led off the proceedings with an attack on the sufficiency of the indictment. He argued that the charges were vague, and failed to provide any indication as to which defendants carried out which alleged acts of sabotage. Instead, the government's indictment simply stated that details concerning the sabotage were peculiarly within the knowledge of the accused. Justice de Wet, in his flowing red robes beneath a wooden canopy, found the defence arguments convincing. He told Yutar that the indictment seemed to presuppose guilt and provided almost no clue as to the nature of the offences. The indictment, Justice de Wet announced, must be quashed. Got off guard, security officials rushed to re-arrest each of the defendants, except one. Yutar salvaged some favourable publicity for the prosecution by announcing that charges would be dropped against Bob Hepple and that he would be the state's first witness.

In December, the remaining defendants were back in court to hear Yutar read the state's new charges. The defendants were accused of sabotage, ordering munitions, recruiting young men for guerrilla warfare, encouraging invasion for foreign military units, and conspiring to obtain funds for revolution from foreign states. The first accused, Nelson Mandela pleaded, "My Lord, it it not I, but the government that should be in the dock. I plead not guilty." Each of the other defendants in turn entered not guilty pleas as well. Yutar delivered the opening statement for the prosecution:

The accused deliberately and maliciously plotted and engineered the commission of acts of violence and destruction throughout the country. The planned purpose thereof was to bring about in the Republic of South Africa chaos, disorder and turmoil, which would be aggravated, according to their plan, by the operation of thousands of trained guerrilla warfare units deployed throughout the country at various vantage points. Their combined operations were planned to lead to confusion, violent insurrection and rebellion, followed, at the appropriate juncture, by an armed invasion of the country by military units of foreign powers. In the midst of the resulting chaos, turmoil and disorder, it was planned by the accused to set up a provisional revolutionary government to take over the administration and control of this country.

Listening to Yutar's address, defence attorneys realised (as Joel Joffe later recounted in his book, *The State vs. Nelson Mandela: The Trial That Changed South Africa*) that for most of the accused the only possible verdict was 'guilty.' The case was therefore, as far as they were concerned, a battle to prevent the death penalty being carried out. The defendants had other goals. Many of them saw the trial as the first and last opportunity to explain to the nation why they felt compelled to do what they did for the sake of South Africa's oppressed.

The first prosecution witness would not be, as earlier promised by Yutar, Bob Hepple. Bob Hepple had fled the country. From the safety of Kenya, Hepple told reporters that he never had any intention of testifying against the defendants, whose aims he shared.

Instead, the star witness for the prosecution was Bruno Mtolo (known in court as Mr. X), a former Umkhonto we Sizwe saboteur. Mtolo told the court that, on orders from the National High Command, he had blown up a municipal office, a power pylon, and an electricity line. He testified that Mandela had given his Natal region MK comrades a pep-talk about their underground missions. He described the workings of bombs, grenades, land mines, and other weapons used by MK saboteurs. Mtolo also testified that he believed that the ANC and MK had become instruments of the Communist Party. He explained that financial and family reasons led him to abandon Umkhonto we Sizwe:

Mtolo: They kept promising that I would be paid, and they were still making promises long after I had given all hope of ever getting anything from them. They didn't care about me nor about the others, the recruits who were arrested.

Yutar: Who did not care about them?

Mtolo: The High Command.

Mtolo's betrayal confused Mandela and the other defendants. In his autobiography, *Long Walk to Freedom*, Mandela wrote he was especially upset with Mtolo's willingness to implicate underground activists who were not charged in the case. Mandela considered this inexcusable.

The other critical piece in the prosecution case was Umkhonto we Sizwe's six-page plan of action, called "Operation Mayibuye," confiscated in the Rivonia raid. The state contended the plan, which called for guerrilla warfare and an invasion of South Africa by supporting foreign military units, had been approved by the ANC executive and was the operating plan of Umkhonto we Sizwe. The defence, on the other hand, contended that Operation Mayibuye was just a draft of a possible plan of action and had not been approved by either MK or the ANC executive. In fact, the defence would argue, many of the defendants (including Nelson Mandela) believed the document to be entirely unrealistic in its goals and plans.

Yutar produced other damning documents, many of which he read dramatically in court. A document marked "Top Secret," in the handwriting of Goldreich and found at Rivonia, discussed revolution and mentioned possible support from the people in the USSR, China, Germany, and Yugoslavia, among other countries. Methods of obtaining weapons, including explosives, were outlined in some detail. Documents such as these shocked many trial observers, but the defendants largely viewed their production with indifference. The defendants were ready to admit that they talked openly about sabotage and armed struggle.

Many of the prosecution witnesses in the Rivonia trial were ANC or MK recruits who testified only after enduring tough questioning while in detention, often in solitary confinement. Some of the recruits were physically mistreated. Knowing that their release from detention and escape from future prosecution depended on providing trial testimony that satisfied the demands of police and prosecutors, how reliable can their testimony be? From the standpoint of the defence, the answer was – not very reliable at all. In his book about the Rivonia trial, defence attorney Joel Joffe entitles a chapter of his book, "Unreliable Prosecution Witnesses."

Joffe provides numerous examples of witnesses lying or shading the truth to fill what would otherwise be weaknesses in the state's case. In one case, witness Cyril Davids, an attendee at a MK training camp, testified (incredibly, in the defence view) that defendant Denis Goldberg ended virtually every training lecture, whether on the use of duplicating machines or instruction in judo, by specifically telling them that their new skill would be used for guerrilla warfare. Another witness, the owner of a private taxi service, testified that he drove several saboteurs to an electricity sub-station and, after dropping them off, saw a flash and heard an explosion. While the defence conceded the taxi driver's testimony was largely accurate, it said that he wrongly placed defendant Raymond Mhlaba (a defendant for whom the state had little other incriminating evidence) in the back seat of his taxi. In fact, as the evidence would later show, Mhlaba wasn't even in the country at the time the sub-station was sabotaged.

For some defendants, including Mandela, Sisulu, Mbeki, and Goldberg, the prosecution's evidence of guilt was strong or overwhelming. In the case of Goldberg, for example, several manufacturers and merchants testified that Goldberg had visited their factories and shops making inquiries about orders of large quantities of parts, such as castings, that had application only in weapon construction. For Goven Mbeki, thirteen separate documents directly implicated him in sabotage planning. For defendants Motsoaledi and Mlangeni, the evidence of guilt was less compelling, but likely to be sufficient given the political circumstances of the trial. Witnesses identified both men as involved either in the training of recruits or the transportation of recruits to receive training. For the other four defendants, the prosecution's cases ranged from weak to virtually non existent. As mentioned above, the evidence connecting Mhlaba to sabotage of a sub-station was questionable at best. Ahmed Kathrada, the lone Indian among the defendants, was captured at Rivonia and said by a witness to have drafted a couple of pamphlets and taped a broadcast for ANC radio. Essentially the only evidence of Rusty Bernstein's guilt came from a witness who claimed to have seen Bernstein on the roof of a Rivonia building helping to erect a radio antenna. And for attorney James Kantor, the most incriminating, if it can be called that, evidence was that his office at the law firm might have been used by other persons in a manner that violated communication bans that they were subject to. Justice de Wet found the evidence against Kantor so convincing that, at the conclusion of the prosecution case, he dismissed all charges against him.

The Defence Case

After the state rested its case, the defence had five weeks to prepare for its presentation of evidence. When court convened on April 23, 1964, Bram Fischer delivered an opening statement. Fischer admitted that seven of the ten remaining defendants (except Bernstein, Kathrada, and Goldberg) were members of the National High Command of Umkhonto we Sizwe, but denied that the High Command had made a decision to embark on a course of guerrilla warfare. "Operation Mayibuye," Fischer said, "had not been adopted, and would not have been adopted while their was some chance of having their objectives achieved by the combination of mass political struggle and sabotage." Fischer finished his address by announcing that the defence case would commence with a statement from the dock by Nelson Mandela.

Mandela chose to give a statement from the dock, even though forgoing cross-examination meant his testimony would be given little weight, because, in his words "I did not want to be limited" to the question-answer format in explaining why he and others found it necessary to undertake a campaign of sabotage against the South African government. Joel Joffe said the defence team recognised that the usual form of testimony would mean Mandela's arguments would lose power as they came out in a jumble of bits and pieces. For two weeks, Mandela had spent nights in his cell drafting his unapologetic speech, a speech that Bram Fischer worried might earn him the death penalty.

The decision to not put Mandela on the stand caught Percy Yutar by surprise. He jumped up from the prosecutor's table to cry, "My Lord! My Lord, I think you should warn the accused that what he says from the dock has far less weight than if he submitted himself to cross-examination." Justice de Wet looked at the prosecutor dryly and said, "I think, Mr. Yutar, that the counsel for the defence have sufficient experience to advise their clients without your assistance." Mandela began speaking in a quiet, even voice. He continue reading for the next four hours. "I am the first accused," Mandela said, and began telling the story of his life, the reasons he joined the struggle for racial equality, and gradually arrived at the conclusion that non-violent protest must give way to more violent approaches if the goals of a multi-racial democracy in South Africa were ever to be achieved:

"At the beginning of June 1961, after a long and anxious assessment of the South African situation, I, and some colleagues, came to the conclusion that as violence in this country was inevitable, it would be unrealistic and wrong for African leaders to continue preaching peace and non-violence at a time when the Government met our peaceful demands with force. This conclusion was not easily arrived at. It was only when all else had failed, when all channels of peaceful protest had been barred to us, the decision was made to embark on violent forms of political struggle, and to form Umkhonto we Sizwe."

Mandela concluded his speech by announcing that he was ready to make the ultimate sacrifice for his cause:

"During my lifetime I have dedicated myself to this struggle of the African people. I have fought against white domination, and I have fought against black domination. I have cherished the ideal of a democratic and free society in which all persons live together in harmony and with equal opportunities. It is an ideal which I hope to live for and to achieve. But if needs be, it is an ideal for which I am prepared to die."

In his autobiography, he describes the scene in the Pretoria courtroom. "The silence seemed to stretch for many minutes. But in fact it lasted probably no more than thirty seconds, and then from the gallery I heard what sounded like a great sigh, a deep, collective 'ummmm,' followed by the cries of women."

Justice de Wet turned to Bram and announced in a gentle voice, "You may call your next witness." Walter Sisulu, former Secretary General of the ANC and a member of MK's National High Command, took the stand. Sisulu testified that Operation Mayibuye was the brain child of Arthur Goldreich, a member of the High Command and a former member of the Israeli underground movement. Sisulu said that the plan had not been adopted, in part because more time was needed to condition the masses. The ANC and Umkhonto, Sisulu also told the court, were separate organisations. He testified that he agreed sabotage was necessary, but insisted that the choice of targets makes the position perfectly clear that the intention was not to injure anybody at all. Pressed on this point by Justice de Wet, who pointed to the death of a passer-by when a bomb exploded at a post office, Sisulu conceded that accidents could happen, despite the precautions Umkhonto tried to take. In five days of cross-examination, Yutar tried to link the ANC and Umkhonto to the Communist Party and pushed Sisulu to identify others who played key roles in underground organisations. Despite warnings from the bench, Sisulu refused to name names.

Over the course of the next week, each of the other seven defendants took the stand, with five (Kathrada, Mhlaba, Bernstein, Mbeki, and Goldberg) subjecting themselves to cross-examination and two (Motsoaledi and Mlangeni) offering, like Mandela, prepared statements. For the several defendants for whom conviction was all but was certain that their time on the stand was an opportunity to explain to the nation why they did what they did. Elias Motsoaledi's brief statement provided one of the more moving moments of the trial. He ended his prepared remarks by telling the court, "What I did brought me no personal gain. What I did, I did for my people and because I thought it was the only way left to help my people. That is all I have to say." But he did have one more thing to say. Looking at the judge, Motsoaledi said: "In addition, my Lord, I want to say that I was assaulted by the Security Branch in an attempt to make me make a statement." For the three defendants (Kathrada, Mhlaba, and Bernstein), for whom conviction was in some doubt testifying offered a chance to rebut whatever weak evidence the prosecution had presented that tied them either to the sabotage or conspiracy charges. Raymond Mhlaba did himself no favour on the stand, according to Joel Joffe, who described the slow-answering, slow-moving man as having made a rather unfortunate impression in the box. On the other hand, Rusty Bernstein was an ideal witness, gave clear, concise answers in a polite and unruffled manner while conceding nothing. His testimony, quite likely, spared him the fate of the other defendants.

Closing Speeches, Verdict, and Sentence

Closing arguments began in the Rivonia trial on May 20. Percy Yutar, for the state, said: "Every particular allegation in the indictment has been proved. There is not a single material allegation in the opening address that has not been proved. On the evidence it is clear that without the action of the police, South Africa might have found itself in a bloody civil war."

Three weeks later, Justice de Wet announced his verdict. Only Rusty Bernstein was acquitted. Ahmed Kathrada was found guilty on one of the four counts. The other defendants are found guilty on all counts. Justice de Wet told the assembled courtroom that he would deal with the question of sentencing the next morning. He released a 72-page summary of the evidence with findings. Justice de Wet concluded, among other things, that beyond doubt Nelson Mandela had been the leading spirit behind the creation of Umkhonto we Sizwe and that Operation Mayibuye comprised a detailed plan for waging guerrilla war intended to culminate in full scale revolt against the Government of South Africa.

There was, however, one confrontation left for the trial. The defence asked to present testimony in mitigation of sentence from Alan Paton, author of the bestselling book, "Cry, the Beloved Country." Paton, a respected member of South Africa's moribund Liberal Party, commanded a huge following both in South Africa and the world as a whole. A packed courtroom awaited his testimony, included numerous representatives from foreign embassies and consulates. Paton told the court that he testified out of a sense of duty because he love his country and his belief that sparing the defendant's lives was very important to their future. Paton did not apologise for what the defendants did, but called them men of courage with a deep devotion to their people. "They have no choice," he said, "but either to bow their heads and submit, or to resist by force."

At times during Paton's testimony, Justice de Wet seemed barely to be listening. His mind had been made up. For weeks, international pressure to spare the defendants' lives in the form of U. N.

resolutions, protests, and secret diplomatic communications had been building. After asking the defendants to rise, Justice de Wet pronounced sentence. "I have decided not to impose the supreme penalty," the judge said, "even though it would normally be the proper penalty for the crime." He concluded his brief statement: "The sentence in the case of all of the accused will be one – life imprisonment."

Nelson Mandela and the other defendants, who had all decided that they would not appeal if sentenced to death, broke into smiles. They would live! Mandela gave a thumbs-up sign to the his supporters. Minutes later, the defendants were hustled into a van. As they drove off, to what for each would be more than two decades of imprisonment, the crowd in the streets outside the courthouse shouted, "Amandla! Nkosi Sikelel iAfrica!" Mandela answered by sticking his clenched fist through the bars of the van's window.

Epilogue

Nelson Mandela spent the next eighteen years in a prison on Robben Island, just off Cape Town. He worked in a lime quarry and was allowed one letter and one visitor every six months. In 1982, authorities transferred Mandela and four other Rivonia defendants (Sisulu, Mlangeni, Mhlaba, and Kathrada) to Pollsmoor Prison in suburban Cape Town.

The winds of change began to sweep South Africa in 1985. Denis Goldberg became the first of the Rivonia defendants to be released from prison. President P. W. Botha offered Mandela a deal – renounce violence and be free. Mandela refused the offer: "Only free men can negotiate, a prisoner cannot enter into contracts." In November of 1985, the National Party government entered into secret negotiations with Mandela for what, it was hoped, might be an eventual transition to a multi-racial government.

By the beginning of 1990, only Mandela among the Rivonia defendants remained imprisoned, now at a bungalow in Victor Verster prison where he continued his secret negotiations. In February 1990, President F. W. de Klerk announced the release of Nelson Mandela. The next year, Mandela was elected president of the ANC.

In April 1994, South Africans of all races went to the polls. The ANC won 62% of the vote and on May 10, Nelson Mandela took the oath of office as the first black President of South Africa.

Nelson Mandela

Born: July 18, 1918

South African black nationalist leader and statesman.

The son of a Xhosa chief, Mandela studied law at the University of Witwatersrand and in 1944 joined the African National Congress (ANC). After the Sharpeville massacre (1960), he abandoned his nonviolent stance and helped found the "Spear of the Nation," the ANC's military wing. Arrested in 1962, he was sentenced to life imprisonment. He retained wide support among South Africa's black population and became an international cause célèbre. Released by Pres. F.W. de Klerk in 1990, he replaced Oliver Tambo as president of the ANC in 1991. In 1993 Mandela and de Klerk were awarded the Nobel Peace Prize for their efforts to end apartheid and bring about the transition to nonracial democracy. In 1994, he was elected president in the country's first universal suffrage elections; by the time he stepped down in 1999, Mandela was the most universally respected figure of postcolonial Africa.

II. The Impeachment Trial of President *William Clinton*

In 1999, for the second time in United States history, the Senate conducted an impeachment trial of a President. The acquittal of William Jefferson Clinton on February 12 came as no great surprise, given the near party-line vote on impeachment charges in the House of Representatives leading to the trial.

Despite its predictable outcome, the impeachment trial of President Clinton is well worth studying, both for what it says about the failure of the judiciary and political institutions to respond adequately to an unprecedented situation, and what it tells us about the failures of Bill Clinton, the all too human occupant of the nation's highest office. The trial also raises fascinating questions about the distinction between *public* morality and *private* morality.

The Paula Jones Sexual Harassment Suit

The impeachment saga of President Clinton has its origins in a sexual harassment lawsuit brought in Arkansas in May, 1994 by Paula Jones, a former Arkansas state employee. In her suit, Jones alleged that on May 8, 1991, while she helped to staff a state-sponsored management conference at the Excelsior Hotel in Little Rock, a state trooper and member of Governor Clinton's security, Danny Ferguson, approached her and told her that the Governor would like to meet her in his hotel suite. Minutes later, Jones, seeing this as an opportunity to advance her career, took the elevator to Clinton's suite. There, according to her disputed account, Clinton made a series of increasingly aggressive moves, culminating in dropping his pants exposing an erection and then asking Jones to kiss it. Jones claimed that she stood and told the Governor, "I'm not that kind of girl." As she left, Clinton stopped her by the door and said, "You're a smart girl, let's keep this between ourselves." (There is strong reason to question Jones's story, as Clinton's security guard reported that Jones seemed pleased when

she left the hotel room and that anything that happened inside appeared to be consensual.)

Lawyers for Clinton argued that the Jones suit would distract him from the important tasks of his office and should not be allowed to go forward while he occupied the White House. Clinton's immunity claim eventually reached the United States Supreme Court. The Court ruled unanimously in May, 1997 against the President, and allowed discovery in the case to proceed. As Federal Appeals Court Judge (and Reagan appointee) Richard A. Posner noted in *An Affair of State: The Investigation, Impeachment, and Trial of President Clinton*, that the Court's inept, unpragmatic, and backward-looking decision in Clinton vs Jones, and an earlier decision by the Court upholding the constitutionality of the act authorising the appointment of independent counsels had major consequences:

"Clinton's affair with Monica Lewinsky, an affair intrinsically devoid of significance to anyone except Lewinsky, would have remained a secret from the public. The public would not have been worse for not knowing about it. There would have been no impeachment inquiry, no impeachment, no concerns about the motives behind the President's military actions against terrorists and rogue states in the summer and fall of 1998, no spectacle of the United States Senate play-acting at adjudication. The Supreme Court's decisions created a situation that led the President and his defenders into the pattern of cornered-rat behaviour that engendered a constitutional storm and that may have embittered American politics, weakened the Presidency, distracted the federal government from essential business, and undermined the rule of law."

As a result of the Supreme Court's action, Judge Susan Weber Wright allowed discovery to proceed in the Paula Jones lawsuit. Judge Wright ruled that lawyers for Jones, in order to help prove her sexual harassment claim, could inquire into any sexual relationships that Clinton might have with subordinates either as Governor of Arkansas or as President of the United States. A critical moment in the cascade of events that would eventually lead to impeachment came on December 5, 1997 when Jones's lawyers submitted a list of women that they would like to depose. Monica Lewinsky's name was also included on the list.

The President and Monica Lewinsky

Monica Lewinsky came to Washington in July 1995 to work as a White House intern at age 21, newly graduated from Lewis and Clark College in Portland. In her first few months on the job, the aggressive and sexually experienced Lewinsky met and flirted with the President, but no opportunities for close personal contact arose. In November 1995, however, Lewinsky was assigned to the West Wing and she soon found herself alone with Clinton. He asked if he could kiss Lewinsky. She quickly consented. Later that evening, the two would have the first of what eventually would be ten sexual encounters over a sixteen-month period. After eight of the encounters had taken place, in April 1996, Clinton's deputy chief of staff, most likely aware of the threat the young intern posed, reassigned Lewinsky to the a position in the Department of Defence. The following month Clinton told a disappointed Lewinsky that he was ending the relationship, but he revived it briefly in early 1997.

Theencountersfollowedapredictablepattern. Generally, theyoccurred on weekend mornings in and around the Oval Office (including a study, a hallway, and a bathroom), when few people except Clinton's personal secretary, Betty Currie, would be around the West Wing. Although many private meetings between the two involved no sexual activity. When they did, they generally included Lewinsky fellating

the President and the President fondling her breasts and genitalia. On three occasions, Lewinsky performed oral sex while the President talked on the phone. Lewinsky told Clinton she would like to have vaginal intercourse with him, but he resisted. He also terminated the oral sex sessions before ejaculation until their last two encounters.

When Clinton again told Lewinsky in May 1997 that their sexual relationship was over, she redoubled efforts that began the previous year to enlist the President's assistance in finding employment. Lewinsky received a job offer from U. N. Ambassador Bill Richardson several months later, but she turned it down, preferring to find private sector employment. Clinton golfing buddy and power broker Vernon Jordan, acting at what he presumed to be the President's request through Betty Currie, met with Lewinsky to discuss employment possibilities in November 1997.

Less than two weeks after Lewinsky's name appeared on the Jones deposition list, Clinton told her the news. He advised her that filing an affidavit might avoid the necessity of a deposition and he reminded her of their "cover story" for her frequent trips to Oval Office – that she was just delivering documents. Two days after discussing the matter with Clinton, Lewinsky received a subpoena to appear for a deposition in January 1998. She called Vernon Jordan, who again met her and referred her to an attorney, who proceeded to draft an affidavit that reflected her denial of any sexual involvement with the President.

Just after Christmas, Lewinsky spoke again with Clinton, raising her concern that the subpoena had requested that she bring to the deposition any gifts that she had received from him. Although Clinton apparently informed Lewinsky that she was obligated to give the lawyers for Jones any gifts in her possession, a call came later that day from Currie, indicating that she understood Lewinsky

had some items she'd like to give her for safekeeping. (Currie, in her testimony, disagreed with Lewinsky's version of events and claimed that the call about the presents came from Lewinsky, not her.) Currie drove to Lewinsky's home and carted away a box of Clinton gifts and put them under her bed.

In early January 1998, Lewinsky signed an affidavit, with the intent of filing it for the Jones case, claiming her relationship with the President was non-sexual. The day after Lewinsky showed the affidavit to Vernon Jordan, Jordan made a call to Ronald Perelman, a friend and member of the Board of Directors of Revlon, encouraging him to hire Lewinsky. The job offer from Revlon came just two days later.

Linda Tripp Gets Involved

The source of the information that put Monica Lewinsky's name on the deposition list for the Jones case was Linda Tripp. Tripp had served in the Bush White House, and was held over in her job when Clinton became president in 1993. Tripp came to despise Clinton. In 1996, when she considered how to expose what she considered to be West Wing scandals, she contacted a conservative literary agent and self-described Clinton-hater, Lucianne Goldberg. Goldberg urged Tripp to write an expose, but at that time Tripp's concern with keeping her job caused her to reject the suggestion.

Tripp's name came to public attention in August 1997 when it appeared in a Newsweek article in which she recalled running into a White House volunteer, Kathleen Willey, shortly after Willey had been kissed and fondled by Clinton in his private office. (Willey, according to Tripp, was "happy and joyful" and the incident was "not a case of sexual harassment.") Paula Jones's lawyers, of course, took note of Tripp's account and undoubtedly determined at that time to add Tripp to their list of potential witnesses.

Months before the Willey story broke, however, Tripp learned from her then-friend, Monica Lewinsky that she was having an affair with the President. Tripp told the reporter for Newsweek, Michael Isikoff, when he approached her to ask about Willey's encounter with Clinton that the better story involved a White House intern, who she left unnamed. Tripp, partly for her own self-defence and partly out of a desire to damage the President's reputation, began secretly taping (in violation of the state law of her home state of Maryland) her own conversations with Lewinsky with a $100 recorder she picked up from a nearby Radio Shack.

During one of her taped conversations with Lewinsky in November 1997, Tripp learned that her friend had in her closet a blue dress that still bore the semen stain from a sexual encounter with the President some nine months earlier. Tripp excitedly called Michael Isikoff with the remarkable news, and urged that the reporter have the dress DNA tested. Isikoff pointed out an obvious problem – even if Newsweek could somehow obtain the dress, the test would be meaningless without a sample of Clinton's DNA and how could the magazine get that? Tripp, however, continued to take an active interest in preserving the semen evidence, urging Lewinsky not to have the dress dry cleaned – as she had planned – for a family occasion because it might be useful for her own "protection" and, besides, the dress made her look really fat.

In early January 1998, at the encouragement of Luciane Goldberg and backers of the Jones lawsuit (who, by this time, had been filled in by Tripp on details of the Lewinsky matter), Tripp contacted Kenneth Starr's Office of Independent Counsel. Tripp told Starr's staff all she knew about the Lewinsky-Clinton scandal and presented them with a collection of damaging tapes of her private conversations with Lewinsky.

The Starr Investigation

By late 1997, despite the several year long "Whitewater" investigation costing tens of millions of dollars, the Office of Independent Counsel (OIC) failed to produce the necessary substantial and credible evidence of an impeachable offence that would justify referring the matter to Congress for further action. It seemed only a matter of weeks before the OIC would be forced to close its far-reaching effort to identify wrongdoing by the President. The removal of Independent Counsel Robert Fiske, a moderate Republican, and his replacement by a three-judge panel headed by David Sentelle (a Reagan appointee and protege of Senator Jesse Helms) with conservative Kenneth Starr was a key turning point in the investigation. Starr had no hesitation about aggressively taking the investigation in a new direction.

About the same time, Judge Wright appeared ready to dismiss Paula Jones's sexual harassment suit after testimony in her deposition proved inconsistent with her initial pleadings. (For example, in her pleadings Jones claimed that the incident at the Excelsior Hotel took place after 2:30, but in her deposition she placed the encounter in the morning after evidence made clear that the Governor had returned to his mansion after the luncheon at the hotel.) The judge also seemed angered and frustrated by leaks of salacious details in the press, in obvious defiance of her gag order, and that presented a second justification for dismissal. The President's camp had every reason to be confident that the case would never go to trial, if they could prevent any new bombshells about Clinton's sexual activities with subordinates.

In January 1998, it all blew up. According to the Starr Report eventually submitted to Congress, that month the OIC received information that Monica Lewinsky was attempting to influence the testimony of one of the witnesses in the Jones investigation (Tripp) and that Ms. Lewinsky herself was prepared to provide false information under oath in that lawsuit. The Report added that Ms. Lewinsky had spoken to the President about being subpoenaed to testify in the Jones suit. Based on these representations, and a "sting tape" of a conversation between Tripp and Lewinsky, the OIC sought and obtained permission from Attorney General Reno to expand his investigation to encompass the Lewinsky affair. In seeking permission from Reno, the OIC neglected to mention its prior contacts with lawyers for Paula Jones, including Starr's own previous discussions with Jones's lawyers on the immunity issue that reached the Supreme Court. Had the OIC disclosed these contacts, a conflict concern might have either resulted in their request being turned down, or a new independent counsel appointed.

On January 16, the day before the President would be deposed in the Jones case, authorisation for the expanded investigation came from

Janet Reno. That afternoon, acting in concert with Linda Tripp, who had invited Lewinsky to the food court of the Pentagon City Mall for lunch, FBI agents acting for the OIC seized Lewinsky and escorted her to room 1012 in the Ritz-Carlton Hotel. There OIC lawyers would–for the next eleven hours–press her to cooperate in their investigation by agreeing to wear a wire and secretly record her conversations with President Clinton. Despite warnings that she could face up to 27 years in prison for perjury and obstruction of justice (in fact, two years would be a far more likely punishment), Lewinsky refused. Her decision might well have saved the Clinton presidency.

The next day, lawyers for Paula Jones, having been fully briefed on the details of the Lewinsky affair, threw a series of questions at the President during his deposition that left him surprised and, at times, flustered. Clinton, however, generally stuck to his script and continued to deny the existence of a sexual relationship with Lewinsky. In fact, the President even denied being alone with Lewinsky.

Back in his Oval Office on the following day, Clinton discussed the Lewinsky affair with Betty Currie in a manner that strongly suggested an attempt to influence her future statements about her boss's relationship with the young intern. He told his personal secretary, "We were never really alone. You could see and hear everything. Monica came on to me, and I never touched her, right?" Clinton would later spin the discussion as an attempt to refresh his recollection about his relationship with Lewinsky – a wildly implausible explanation, given that some of the questions he asked Currie, she was in no position to answer.

The American public first learned of allegations of a Clinton affair with Lewinsky on January 21, 1998. The President stuck with his "deny-it-all" strategy, at one point memorably wagging his finger in a televised interview and insisting, "I did not have sexual relations with that woman, Miss Lewinsky." Several of Clinton's aides were (including Sidney Blumenthal, who was later deposed in the Senate trial) assured by the President that his relationship with Lewinsky was non-sexual, appeared in various venues to denounce Starr's investigations as "a puritanical witch hunt" and to call into question Lewinsky's credibility.

The denials from the White House continued till summer, when the President became aware of the fact that his semen stain remained on the blue dress that Monica Lewinsky wore into the Oval Office on a February day in 1997, and that Lewinsky had signed an immunity agreement with the Office of Independent Counsel. In the meantime, Starr's office had interviewed Secret Service agents, friends of Lewinsky, examined hundreds of emails and White House telephone records, and listened to dozens of hours of taped conversations between Tripp and Lewinsky.

On August 17, 1998, the President faced a federal grand jury called to consider whether he committed perjury, or otherwise obstructed justice, in the Paula Jones case. Clinton maintained that while he was being as unhelpful as possible to Jones's lawyers in his earlier deposition, he had not actually lied. He insisted on his right to adopt a very narrow (and very odd) definition of "alone," and stated that oral sex was not, in his opinion, "sexual relations" within the meaning of that term as adopted in the Jones case. He conceded that fondling Lewinsky would be "sexual relations" and so, implicitly, denied the former intern's allegation that he had fondled her breast and genitalia on several occasions. He explained his discussion with Currie as an innocent attempt to check his recollection of facts against hers, and denied that Vernon Jordan's job hunting efforts were in any way tied to Lewinsky's decision to file an affidavit falsely denying a sexual relationship with the President. The night, when his exhausting deposition was over, Clinton appeared on national television from the Map Room of the White House to admit, "I did have a relationship with Miss Lewinsky that not appropriate" and to lash out at Kenneth Starr for invading his private life. "It is time to stop the pursuit of personal destruction," the President said, "and get on with our national life."

The House Votes to Impeach

In the days following his grand jury testimony, calls for impeachment mounted. In the House, Republican Majority Whip Tom De Lay called his aides back to Washington from their summer vacations to announce that it would be his mission to drive Bill Clinton from office. "This is going to be the most important thing I do in my political career," he told them, "and I want all of you to dedicate yourselves to it or leave." De Lay arranged a conference call that included most of the House Republican leadership to urge impeachment. Although

Speaker Newt Gingrich initially opposed the idea, by the time the call was over, he had come around to believed that the cause was right.

In the days following Clinton's admission that he had lied to the American public about the Lewinsky affair, many Congressional expressed their disappointment with the President. Vermont Senator Patrick Leahy scolded Clinton: "Bill, you're a fool! You're a damn, damn, damn fool!" California Senator Dianne Feinstein announced that her trust in his credibility has been badly shattered. New York Senator Patrick Moynihan warned, "We can be our own worst enemies if we do not hew to our best standards." In late August 1998, the survival of the Clinton presidency seemed in real doubt.

Kenneth Starr was required by law to present the House with any substantial and credible information that might provide a ground for impeachment. On September 9, Starr piled thirty six boxes of evidence on the Lewinsky scandal into two vans and ordered them driven to Capitol Hill for deposit. Two days later, the Starr Report, a 453-page summary of the evidence against the President was released to the public over the Internet. The report outlined the case for eleven counts against Clinton, including perjury in his Jones and grand jury depositions, obstruction of justice, and one count asserting abuse of office. Late night comics and critics of the President relished the incredibly explicit details of the report, ranging from the fact that the President took calls from Congressman while receiving oral sex to an account of his inserting his cigar in Lewinsky's vagina. The embarrassing details, which were unnecessary to the prosecution case, were seen by some commentators as a spiteful effort by the OIC to debilitate the Clinton presidency.

Responsibility for recommending action on impeachment fell to the House Judiciary Committee and its Chairman, Henry Hyde. (Hyde, meanwhile, had his own problem to manage: reports surfaced that the widely respected septuagenarian congressman had had an affair some thirty years earlier.) The committee voted to release a videotape of Clinton's four hours of testimony before the grand jury, as well as over 7,000 other pages of evidence, including DNA test results, love notes from Lewinsky to the President, transcripts of Lewinsky's conversations with Linda Tripp, and White House phone logs. After pouring over the evidence and listening to its appointed counsel, the Committee, voting 21 to 16 along party lines on October 5, authorised a full impeachment inquiry. Democrats on the committee, arguing that the case came down to "lying about sex," generally favoured censure as an alternative. The Committee's decision was ratified by the full House three days later, with thirty-one Democrats joining the majority.

Mid-term elections on November 3 brought good news for the President. Before the election, Gingrich predicted that Republicans would gain twenty House seats. In fact, they lost five. Despite the losses, widely interpreted as a public vote against impeachment, Hyde determined to press forward with the inquiry, although on a faster timetable. Privately, Hyde thought impeachment was dead, telling Democratic congressman Charles Schumer, "Charlie, don't worry about it. The committee will report out the articles, but they'll die on the House floor." The disappointing election results convinced Bob Livingston to challenge Gingrich for the position of House Speaker. Within hours of Livingston's decision, Gingrich announced his resignation. One week after Gingrich's surprise announcement, there was another big development – Clinton and Paula Jones finally agreed to settle the sexual harassment lawsuit that had caused all the President's miseries.

Over the course of the next month, the Judiciary Committee considered the evidence and sought to separate Clinton's minor transgressions from those that might form the basis for articles of impeachment. The highlight of the committee's hearings came with the testimony of Kenneth Starr. While Republican members asked questions designed to help Starr lay out his case against the President, Democratic members, preferring to put Starr himself on trial, asked questions that supported their goal of portraying Starr as a zealot. Democratic member John Conyers characterised Starr as a federally paid sex policeman. As another part of the process, the Committee drafted a set of 81 questions for the President to answer concerning a series of events relating to the Lewinsky scandal and his prior testimony. The President answered, but in the opinion of Committee Republicans in a quarrelsome, unresponsive way. Frequently, he responded to questions by saying he did not recall something. Irritated by his answers, some undecided House Republicans moved toward favouring impeachment.

After listening to a panel of experts on impeachment and lawyers for the President earlier in the week, the Judiciary Committee voted on December 11 and 12 to approve four articles of impeachment. The next day, Hyde joined Tom De Lay and Majority Leader Richard Armey in calling for the President to resign. Clinton, the same day, tells reporters that the thought never crossed his mind.

The next week, as the President juggled ordering U. S. planes to launch missile strikes on Iraq with phone calls to undecided Republican House members, impeachment moved to a final vote in the House. Adding to the drama was the resignation of Bob Livingston the same day following disclosure of an affair of his own (stemming from an offer by *Hustler* publisher Larry Flynt to pay $1 million for "documentary evidence of illicit sexual relations" involving high-ranking members of Congress). Minority Leader Richard Gephardt rose to ask Livingston to reconsider his decision to step down, telling his colleagues, "We need to stop destroying imperfect people at the alter of an unobtainable morality." When the final vote came, the House approved two of the four impeachment articles sent up by the Judiciary Committee, rejecting Article II, based on perjury in the Jones deposition, and Article IV containing general charges relating to his unresponsive answers to Judiciary Committee questions and abuse of his office.

That evening, December 19, 1998, on the South Lawn of the White House surrounded by Democratic supporters, the President thanked those who voted against the impeachment articles and urged to stop the politics of personal destruction. "We must," he said, "get rid of the poisonous venom of excessive partisanship, obsessive animosity, and uncontrolled anger." Polls taken that week suggested that the American public sided with Clinton, with 60% opposing impeachment.

Trial in the Senate

"Hear, ye! Hear, ye! Hear, ye!" the Senate's sergeant at arms called out on January 7, 1999. "All persons are commanded to keep silent, on pain of imprisonment, while the House of Representatives is exhibiting to the Senate the articles of impeachment against William Jefferson Clinton, President of the United States."

The impeachment trial of the President formally opened before all 100 senators with the reading of the charges against the President and the swearing in of the presiding officer, Chief Justice William Rehnquist, dressed in a black robe with four bright yellow braids on each sleeve, a fashion idea that Rehnquist had taken from a judge in Gilbert and Sullivan's *Iolanthe*.

The next day, the Senate met in a closed session to hammer out a bipartisan plan (passed on a vote of 100 to 0) for procedural rules to govern the trial. Each side would get twenty-four hours to present its case without witnesses. The senators would then have two days for a question-and-answer session, only after that would the Senate vote on motions to dismiss or requests for witnesses.

The House managers, who would prosecute Clinton in the Senate, plotted strategy. A key question they faced was whether to call live witnesses and, if so, how many and which ones. A preliminary list drawn up included many names: the judge in Jones case, Susan Weber Wright, Monica Lewinsky, Secret Service agents, Kathleen Willey (a White House volunteer who claimed to have been groped by Clinton), Vernon Jordan, various Clinton aides, and even New York mayor Rudy Giuliani (who, as a former U. S. attorney, could address the subject of prosecutions of public officials). Senate Majority Leader Trent Lott, and Minority Leader Tom Daschle, were not, however, thrilled at the prospect of live witnesses. They saw live witnesses as a threat to their desire to stage a speedy and dignified trial that would not become an embarrassing national spectacle. Both leaders understood that the prospects of at least a dozen Democratic Senators voting to convict, the minimum necessary for the required two-thirds vote, were exceedingly slim, barring some new shocking revelation about the President's conduct.

The trial got underway in earnest on January 14. "Well, let's begin," the Chief Justice announced, adding, "fight fair." House Manager James Sensenbrenner opened the prosecution case with a monotonous summary of the case that left some Senators, such as Alaska's Ted Stevens, asleep. Other senators, including Joseph Biden, Arlen Specter and Bob Kerry took extensive notes. Following Sensenbrenner, three other managers had somewhat better luck keeping senators alert with a parade of charts, timelines, and video clips aimed at demonstrating a pattern of illegal obstruction of justice. Even Democratic senators conceded that Manager Asa Hutchinson's outlining of the sequence of events in the Lewinsky affair was especially effective. Some appeared to be having second thoughts about their intended votes.

As opening arguments continued for another four hours the next day, senators struggled to remain engaged during what became, in Peter Baker's description in *The Breach*, "A law school seminar on perjury and obstruction of justice." The only break in the tedium came when Iowa's Democratic Senator Tom Harkin stood and shouted, "Mr. Chief Justice, I object." Harkin's objection turned out to be the managers' practice of referring to the senators as "jurors" when in fact their role required them to take account not only the evidence, but also the effect impeachment might have on the nation. Chief Justice Rehnquist generally agreed and told the Manager Bob Barr, "Counsel should refrain from referring to the senators as jurors."

The following day, arguments by the managers focused mostly on whether Clinton's conduct met the constitutional standard of a "high crime" justifying removal. In his address, Henry Hyde insisted that the label of "Clinton-haters" had been attached to the managers, "This is not a question of who we hate; it's a question of what we love. And among the things we love are the rule of law, equal justice before the law, and honour in our public life."

Wheelchair-bound Charles Ruff opened the case for the President on January 19, only hours before President Clinton would deliver his State of the Union Address. Ruff told the senators that the overzealous managers had concocted a witches' brew of charges and were making "a rush to judgment. He accused the managers of fudging the facts to suit their case. He concluded by suggesting that senators were free to find their personal conduct distasteful, but they should ask themselves whether for the first time in their history, the actions of a President have so put at risk the government the framers created that there is only one solution. Continuing arguments for the President the next day, Greg Craig said that Clinton did not commit perjury in his grand jury deposition, but rather was guilty only of nitpicking and arguing with the prosecutors. The task of wrapping up opening arguments for the President's team fell to an ex-senator from Clinton's home state of Arkansas, Daryl Bumpers. Bumpers proved a good choice, as he in his folksy way summed up what he saw as the major problem with the managers' case: "When you hear somebody say, 'This is not about sex,' it's about sex." The punishment, Bumpers argued, is totally out of sync with the charge.

The two-day question-and-answer session became an opportunity for senators to throw softballs to their respective sides. Republican senators turned their questions into Trent Lott, who sent them on to a team of three Republican senators who weeded out the unhelpful questions, and put them in an order suiting the manager's goals. A list of 179 additional proposed questions were left in a binder for any senator willing to "ask" them. Democrats also orchestrated their question-asking, deciding on a strategy of leading with a series of prepared questions, then improvising to best suit the flow of the arguments. Chief Justice Rehnquist asked the questions, first one from the Republicans, then one from the Democrats. One of the few questions to produce any real surprise came from senators John Edwards of North Carolina and Herb Kohl of Wisconsin. The two Democratic senators noted in their question, that both sides had spoken in absolutes while it struck many of them as a closer call. In view of this, Edwards and Kohl asked, "Even if the President engaged in the alleged conduct, can reasonable people disagree with the conclusion that, as a matter of law, he must be convicted and removed from office – yes or no?" Manager Lindsay Graham dismayed many of his Republican colleagues when he answered, "Absolutely." Graham admitted the Constitution gave no definitive answer and said, "If I was sitting where you are, I would probably get down on my knees before I made that decision."

The day after the question-and-answer period, Monica Lewinsky, having been ordered to fly from Los Angeles to Washington to meet with the House managers, reluctantly appeared at the Capitol's Mayflower Hotel to discuss with three congressmen, her possible testimony in the Senate trial. Lewinsky was worried, told a friend, "I'm nervous about what he'll (Starr) do to me if he doesn't get what he wants." Lewinsky, after receiving assurances that her answers were covered by her immunity agreement, answered the managers' questions. The questions ranged from why she kept her stained dress (it made her look fat) to what she thought should happen to Clinton ("I think he should be censured but not removed"). The managers concluded from their interview that Lewinsky would make a great live witness. They narrowed their wish list of witnesses to three –

Lewinsky, Vernon Jordan, and Sidney Blumenthal. The media frenzy surrounding Lewinsky's return to Washington, however, was giving some Republican senators second thoughts whether they wanted her or any other live trial witnesses.

On January 27, the Senate met to vote on a motion by Democratic Senator Harry Byrd of West Virginia to dismiss the impeachment case against the President. When the Chief Justice called for the clerk to call the roll, everyone knew that the motion would fail along nearly strict party lines. It did. The motion was defeated 56 to 44, with only one Democratic senator, Russ Feingold of Wisconsin, not voting with his party. A second roll call vote followed almost immediately on the motion to allow the managers to depose their three witnesses. It passed on the same 56 to 44 vote.

Over the first three days in February, House managers deposed Lewinsky, Jordan, and Blumenthal. Lewinsky's deposition took place in a hotel suite before a throng of over forty attorneys and congressional aides. Under Congressman Edward Bryant's inartful questioning, she proved a dominating and unhelpful witnesses, often answering with just a "yes" or a "no." She described her present feelings toward the President as "mixed" and claimed that she filed her false affidavit in the Jones case for her own interests, not Clinton's. Most observers left the deposition believing that Lewinsky was no victim. Tom Griffin, the Senate's chief lawyer, having witnessed the deposition, described it to Trent Lott as a disaster.

Support for live witnesses collapsed after the Lewinsky deposition. The Senate voted 70 to 30 against issuing Lewinsky a subpoena to testify. Instead, on a 62 to 38 vote, the Senate authorised each side to show video excerpts of deposition testimony by each of the three witnesses. On February 6, the managers projected video images of Lewinsky, Jordan, and Blumenthal on four flat screens at the front of the chamber. Clinton's lawyers did the same, offering an uninterrupted twenty-minute clip of Lewinsky that showed her intelligence and near total control of her questioner.

Closing arguments began two days later. Ruff, for the President, accused the managers of having a vision more focused on retribution than the best interests of the country. Each of the thirteen managers offered reasons to impeach, including Asa Hutchinson who urged the senators to have the political courage to follow the facts despite enormous pressure to ignore them. Hyde, speaking last, ended with the call, "Let right be done."

Senators met behind closed doors to consider their votes. Each senator was alloted fifteen minutes to make a statement. Most attention was focused on a handful of senators whose votes were not clear. Republican John McCain announced that the President deliberately subverted the rule of law and that he would vote guilty on both articles. The one Democrat whose vote was in doubt, Russ Feingold, called the case closed but said, "If we must err, let us err on the side of avoiding divisions, let us err on the side of respecting the will of the people." Feingold would vote to acquit.

On Friday, February 12, 1999, Chief Justice Rehnquist intoned, "The question is on the first article of impeachment. Senators, how say you? Is the respondent, William Jefferson Clinton, guilty or not guilty?" Not guilty, it turned out – fifty-five senators, including ten Republicans, voted to acquit on the perjury count. The vote on the second article was closer, 50 to 50, but still far short of the two-thirds vote required for conviction. Five Republicans voted "not guilty" on the second article relating to obstruction of justice: John Chafee (RI), Susan Collins (ME). Jim Jeffords (VT)., Olympia Snow (ME), and Arlen Specter (PA).

President Clinton read a statement two hours later. He expressed the hope that all Americans there and in Washington and throughout their land will rededicate themselves to the work of serving their nation and building their future together."

Lessons from the Trial

This is a trial that never should have happened. Clinton should have reached an early settlement (or defaulted) in his suit with Jones, which would have happened if he'd been honest with his own lawyers about his sexual history. The Supreme Court should have struck down the independent counsel law as a violation of separation of powers when it had a chance to do so in 1988. The Supreme Court missed a second chance to prevent impeachment when it failed to recognise, in *Clinton vs Jones*, that civil suits against a sitting President had the serious potential to be a major distraction from the President's duties. Clinton should not have trusted Lewinsky to be discreet. Kenneth Starr should not have engaged in a sting operation against the President of the United States, and the Administration should not have engaged in an operation to trash the OIC. Finally, of course, the President should not have lied under oath about his relationship with Monica Lewinsky.

Yet, the trial did happen and what can be learned from the experience? Several things, it turns out. We learned that politics are very likely to determine how one views evidence in impeachment case not a surprising lesson to be sure, but the final votes in both the House and Senate turned out to be *surprisingly* partisan. Moreover, the analysis of academics – people trained to look objectively at evidence – who threw themselves into the impeachment fray was, if anything, even more partisan than that of the politicians.

We learned that the Administration's decision to go on a war footing when allegations of the President's affair with Lewinsky first surfaced proved costly. Relentless attacks by Clinton and his aides on the Office of Independent Counsel and Linda Tripp angered Republicans, polarised debate, and made impeachment by the House inevitable. At the same time, the aggressive approach might have made acquittal in the Senate inevitiable.

We also learned that an impeachment trial is not necessarily a national calamity and might even have some benefits. George W. Bush has shown that the presidency was not seriously weakened by the ordeal. The public might be better off today for having had to think seriously about issues of both private and public morality during the impeachment process. The Clinton-Lewinsky scandal also contributed to a franker national discussion about sex and, by demonstrating how many skeletons exist in the closets of politicians, might cause future elections to turn more on matters of substance than what one of the candidates did in bed sometime in the past.

Finally, as Richard Posner astutely observed in *An Affair of State*, the impeachment of William Clinton had by the dint of its riviting detail made it difficult to take presidents seriously. The destruction of the mystique of the presidency is for those who think that authority depends upon mystery, a consequence to be lamented. But Posner disagrees: "My guess is that they are wrong, that Americans have reached a level of political sophistication at which they can take in stride the knowledge that the nation's political and intellectual leaders are their peers, and not their paragons. The nation does not depend upon the superior virtue of one man."

William Clinton

Born: Aug. 19, 1946, Hope, Arkanas, U.S.

42nd president of the U.S. (1993–2001).

Born as William Jefferson Blythe III shortly after his father's death in a car crash, he later took the last name of his mother's second husband, Roger Clinton. He attended Georgetown University, the University of Oxford (as a Rhodes Scholar), and Yale Law School, then taught law at the University of Arkansas. He served as state attorney general (1977–79) and served several terms as governor (1979–81, 1983–92), during which he reformed Arkansas's educational system and encouraged the growth of industry through favourable tax policies. In 1992, he won the Democratic Party presidential nomination despite charges of personal impropriety; in the subsequent election he defeated the incumbent, Republican George Bush, and independent candidate H. Ross Perot. As President, Clinton obtained Senate ratification of the NAFTA accord in 1993. Along with his wife, Hillary Rodham Clinton, he devised a plan to overhaul the U.S. health care system, but it was rejected by Congress. He committed U.S. forces to a peacekeeping initiative in Bosnia and Herzegovina. In 1994, the Democrats lost control of Congress for the first time since 1954. Clinton responded by offering a deficit-reduction plan while opposing efforts to slow government spending on social programs. He defeated Robert Dole to win reelection in 1996. In 1997, he helped broker a peace agreement in Northern Ireland. He faced renewed charges of personal impropriety, this time involving his relationship with a White House intern, Monica Lewinsky; he denied the charges before a grand jury but ultimately acknowledged "improper relations" in a televised address. In 1998, Clinton became the second President in history to be impeached. Charged with perjury and obstruction of justice, he was acquitted by the Senate in 1999. His two terms saw sustained economic growth and successive budget surpluses, the first in three decades.

12. The Trial of *Susan B. Anthony*

More than any other woman of her generation, Susan B. Anthony saw that all of the legal disabilities faced by American women owed their existence to the simple fact that women lacked the vote. When Anthony, at age 32, attended her first woman's rights convention in Syracuse in 1852, she declared that the right which woman needed above every other, the one indeed which would secure to her all the others, was the right of suffrage. Anthony spent the next fifty-plus years of her life fighting for the right to vote. She would work tirelessly – giving speeches, petitioning Congress and state legislatures, publishing a feminist newspaper, all for a cause that would not succeed until the ratification of the Nineteenth Amendment fourteen years after her death in 1906.

She would, however, once have the satisfaction of seeing her completed ballot drop through the opening of a ballot box. It happened in Rochester, New York on November 5, 1872, and the event and the trial for illegal voting that followed would create a opportunity for Anthony to spread her arguments for women suffrage to a wider audience than ever before.

The Vote

Anthony had been planning to vote long before 1872. She would later state, "I have been resolved for three years to vote at the first election when I had been home for thirty days before." (New York law required legal voters to reside for the thirty days prior to the election in the district where they offered their vote.) Anthony had taken the position and argued it wherever she could that the recently adopted Fourteenth Amendment gave women the constitutional right to vote in federal elections. The Amendment said that all persons born and naturalised in the United States are citizens of the United States, and as citizens were entitled to the "privileges" of citizens of the United

States. To Anthony's way of thinking, those privileges certainly included the right to vote.

On November 1, 1872, Anthony and her three sisters entered a voter registration office set up in a barbershop. The four Anthony women were part of a group of fifty women Anthony had organised to register in her home town of Rochester. As they entered the barbershop, the women saw stationed in the office three young men serving as registrars. Anthony walked directly to the election inspectors and, as one of the inspectors would later testify that the Anthony group demanded that they register them as voters.

The election inspectors refused Anthony's request, but she persisted, quoting the Fourteenth Amendment's citizenship provision and the article from the New York Constitution pertaining to voting, which contained no sex qualification. The registers remained unmoved. Finally, according to one published account, Anthony gave the men an argument that she thought might catch their attention: "If you refuse us our rights as citizens, I will bring charges against you in Criminal Court and I will sue each of you personally for large, exemplary damages!" She added, "I know I can win. I have Judge Selden as a lawyer. There is any amount of money to back me, and if I have to, I will push to the 'last ditch' in both courts."

The stunned inspectors discussed the situation. They sought the advice of the Supervisor of elections, Daniel Warner, who, according to thirty-three-year-old election inspector E. T. Marsh, suggested that they allow the women to take the oath of registry. "Young men," Marsh quoted Warner as saying, "do you know the penalty of law if you refuse to register these names?" Registering the women, the registrars were advised to put the entire onus of the affair on them. Following Warner's advice, the three inspectors voted to allow Anthony and her three sisters were registered to vote in Rochester's eighth ward. Testifying later about the registration process, Anthony

remembered, "It was a full hour of debate between the supervisors, the inspectors, and himself." In all, fourteen Rochester women successfully registered that day, leading to calls in one city paper for the arrest of the voting inspectors who complied with the women's demand. The *Rochester Union and Advertiser* editorialised in its November 4 edition: "Citizenship no more carries the right to vote that it carries the power to fly to the moon. If these women in the Eighth Ward offer to vote, they should be challenged, and if they take the oaths and the Inspectors receive and deposit their ballots, they should all be prosecuted to the full extent of the law."

Soon after the polls opened at the West End News Depot on Election Day, November 5, Anthony and seven or eight other women cast their ballots. Inspectors voted two to one to accept Anthony's vote, and her folded ballot was deposited in a ballot box by one of the inspectors. Inspector E. T. Marsh testified later as to feeling caught between a rock and a hard place: "Decide which way we might, we were liable to prosecution. We were expected to make an infallible decision of a question in which some of the best minds of the country are divided." Seven or eight more women of Rochester successfully voted in the afternoon. Anthony's vote went to U. S. Grant and other Republicans, based on that party's promise to give the demands of women a respectful hearing. Later that day, Anthony would write of her accomplishment to her close friend and fellow suffragist, Elizabeth Cady Stanton:

Dear Mrs Stanton

Well I have been & gone & done it!! Positively voted the Republican ticket straight this a.m. at 7 O'clock & swore my vote in that – was registered on Friday....then on Sunday others some twenty or thirty other women tried to register, but all were refused....Amy Post was rejected & she will immediately bring action for that and Hon Henry R. Selden will be our Counsel – he has read up the law & all of our arguments & is satisfied that we our right & ditto the Old Judge Selden, his elder brother. So we are in for a fine agitation in Rochester on the question – I hope the morning's telegrams will tell of many women all over the country trying to vote. It is splendid that without any concert of action so many should have moved here so impromptu.

The Democratic paper is out against us strong & that scared the Dem's on the registry board. How I wish you were here to write up the funny things said & done. When the Democrat said my vote should not go in the box – one Republican said to the other – What do you say Marsh? I say put it in! So do I said Jones, "We'll fight it out on this line if it takes all winter." If only now all the women suffrage would work to this end of enforcing the existing constitution – supremacy of national law over state law – what strides we might make this winter. But I'm awfully tired for five days I have been on the constant run but to splendid purpose. So all right, I hope you voted too.

Affectionately,

Susan B. Anthony

Arrest and Indictment

The votes of Susan Anthony and other Rochester women was a major topic of conversation in the days that followed. In a November 11 letter to Sarah Huntington, Anthony wrote: "Our papers are discussing pro & con everyday." Anthony occupied much of her time meeting with lawyers to discuss a planned lawsuit by some of the women whose efforts to register or vote were rejected.

Meanwhile, a Rochester salt manufacturer and Democratic poll watcher named Sylvester Lewis filed a complaint charging Anthony with casting an illegal vote. Lewis had challenged both Anthony's registration and her subsequent vote. United States Commissioner William C. Storrs acted upon Lewis's complaint by issuing a warrant for Anthony's arrest on November 14. The warrant charged Anthony with voting in a federal election without having a lawful right to vote and in violation of section 19 of an act of Congress enacted in 1870, commonly called The Enforcement Act. The Enforcement Act carried a maximum penalty of $500 or three years imprisonment.

The actual arrest of Anthony was delayed for four days to allow time for Storrs to discuss the possible prosecution with the U. S. Attorney for the Northern District of New York. On November 18, a United States deputy marshal showed up at the Anthony home on Madison Street in Rochester, where he was greeted by one of Susan's sisters. At the request of the deputy, Anthony's sister summoned Susan to the parlour. Susan Anthony had been expecting her visitor. As Anthony would later tell audiences, she had previously received word from Commissioner Storrs to call at his office. Anthony's response was characteristically plainspoken: "I sent word to him that I had no social acquaintance with him and didn't wish to call on him."

At the May meeting of the National Women's Suffrage Association, Anthony described what happened when the deputy marshal, a young man in beaver hat and kid gloves (paid for by taxes gathered from women), came to see her:

He sat down. He said it was pleasant weather. He hemmed and hawed and finally said, "Mr. Storrs wanted to see me" What for?" I asked. "To arrest you," said he. "Is that the way you arrest men?" "No." Then I demanded that I should be arrested properly. (According to another account, Anthony at this point held out her wrists and demanded to be handcuffed.) My sister desiring to go with me he proposed that he should go ahead and I follow with her. This I refused, and he had to go with me. In the (horse-drawn) car he took out his pocketbook to pay fare. I asked if he did that in his official capacity. He said yes; he was obliged to pay the fare of any criminal he arrested. Well, that was the first cents worth I ever had from Uncle Sam.

Anthony was escorted to the office of Commissioner Storrs, described by Anthony as the same dingy little room where, in the olden days, fugitive slaves were examined and returned to their masters. Upon arriving, Anthony was surprised to learn that among those arrested for their activities on November 5 were not only the fourteen other women voters, but also the ballot inspectors who had authorised their votes.

Anthony's lawyers refused to enter a plea at the time of her arrest, and Storrs scheduled a preliminary examination for November 29. At the hearing on the 29th, complainant Sylvestor Lewis and Eighth Ward Inspectors appeared as the chief witnesses against Anthony. Anthony was questioned at the hearing by one of her lawyers, John Van

Voorhis. Van Voorhis tried to establish through his questions that Anthony believed that she had a legal right to vote and therefore had not violated the 1870 Enforcement Act, which prohibited only willful and knowing illegal votes. Anthony testified that she had sought legal advice from Judge Henry R. Selden prior to casting her vote, but that Selden said he had not studied the question. Van Voorhis asked: "Did you have any doubt yourself of your right to vote?" Anthony replied, "Not a particle." Storrs adjourned the case to December 23.

After listening to legal arguments in December, Commissioner Storrs concluded that Anthony probably violated the law. When Anthony, alone among those charged with Election Day offences refused bail, Storrs ordered her held in the custody of a deputy marshal until the grand jury had a chance to meet in January and consider issuing an indictment. Anthony saw the commissioner's decision as a ticket to Supreme Court review, and began making plans with her lawyers to file a petition for a writ of habeas corpus. In a December 26 letter, Anthony wrote confidently, "We shall be rescued from the Marshall hands on a writ of habeas corpus case carried to the Supreme Court of the U. S. – the speediest process of getting there." Already letters were coming in with contributions to her Defence Fund. She was anxious to put the money to use.

By early January, Anthony was already trying to make political hay out of her arrest. She sent off "hundreds of papers" concerning her arrest to suffragist friends and politicians. She still, however, found her situation difficult to comprehend: "I never dream of the U. S. officers prosecuting me for voting – thought only that if I was refused I should bring action against the inspectors. But Uncle Sam waxes wroth with holy indignation at such violation of his laws!!"

Anthony's attorney, Henry Selden asked a U. S. District Judge in Albany, Nathan Hall, to issue a writ of habeas corpus ordering the release of Anthony from the marshal's custody. Hall denied Selden's request and said he would allow defendant to go to the Supreme Court of the United States. The judge then raised Anthony's bail from $500 to $1000. Anthony again refused to pay. Selden, however, decided to pay Anthony's bail with money from his own bank account. In the courtroom hallway following the hearing Anthony's other lawyer, John Van Voorhis, told Anthony that Selden's decision to pay her bail meant: "You've lost your chance to get your case before the Supreme

Court." Shaken by the news, Anthony confronted her lawyer, demanding that he explain why he paid her bail. "I could not see a lady I respected put in jail," Selden answered.

A disappointed Anthony still had a trial to face. On January 24, 1873, a grand jury of twenty men returned an indictment against Anthony charging her with "knowingly, wrongfully, and unlawfully" voting for a member of Congress without having a lawful right to vote, the said Susan B. Anthony being then and there a person of the female sex." The trial was set for May.

On the Stump

Anthony saw the four months until her trial as an opportunity to educate the citizens of Rochester and surrounding counties on the issue of women suffrage. She took to the stump, speaking in town after town on the topic, "Is it a crime for a citizen of the United States to vote?"

By mid-May, Anthony's exhausting lecture tour had taken her to every one of the twenty-nine post-office districts in Monroe County. To many in her audience, Anthony was the picture of "sophisticated refinement and sincerity." The fifty-two-year-old suffragist delivered her earnest speeches dressed in a grey silk dress with a white lace collar. Her smoothed hair was twisted neatly into a tight knot. She would look at her audience, ranging from a few dozen to over a hundred persons, and begin:

Friends and Fellow-citizens – I stand before you tonight, under indictment for the alleged crime of having voted at the last Presidential election, without having a lawful right to vote. It shall be my work this evening to prove to you that in thus voting, I not only committed no crime, but simply exercised my citizen's right, guaranteed to me and all United States citizens by the National Constitution, beyond the power of any State to deny.

In her address, Anthony quoted the Declaration of Independence, the U. S. Constitution, the New York Constitution, James Madison, Thomas Paine, the Supreme Court, and several of the leading Radical Republican senators of the day to support her contention that women had a legal right as citizens to vote. She argued that natural law, as well as a proper interpretation of the Civil War Amendments, gave women the power to vote, as in this passage suggesting that women, having been in a state of servitude, were enfranchised by the recently enacted Fifteenth Amendment extending the vote to ex-slaves:

"And yet one more authority; that of Thomas Paine, than whom not one of the Revolutionary patriots more ably vindicated the principles upon which our government is founded.

The right of voting for representatives is the primary right by which other rights are protected. To take away this right is to reduce man to a state of slavery; for slavery consists in being subject to the will of another; and he who has not cast a vote in the election of representatives is in this case.

Is anything further needed to prove woman's condition of servitude sufficiently orthodox to entitle her to the guaranties of the Fifteenth Amendment? Is there a man who will not agree with me, that to talk of freedom without the ballot, is mockery – is slavery – to the women of this Republic, precisely as New England's orator Wendell Phillips, at the close of the late war, declared it to be to the newly emancipated black men?"

Anthony ended her hour-long lectures by frankly attempting to influence potential jurors to vindicate her in her upcoming trial:

"We appeal to the women everywhere to exercise their too long neglected citizen's right to vote. We appeal to the inspectors of elections everywhere to receive the votes of all United States citizens as it is their duty to do. We appeal to United States commissioners and marshals to arrest the inspectors who reject the names and votes of United States citizens, as it is their duty to do, and leave those alone who, like our eighth ward inspectors, perform their duties faithfully and well.

We ask the juries to fail to return verdicts of guilty against honest, law-abiding, tax-paying United States citizens for offering their votes at our elections. Or against intelligent, worthy young men, inspectors of elections, for receiving and counting such citizens votes.

We ask the judges to render true and unprejudiced opinions of the law, and wherever there is room for a doubt to give its benefit on the side of liberty and equal rights to women, remembering that the true rule of interpretation under our national constitution, especially since its amendments, is that anything for human rights is constitutional, everything against human right unconstitutional.

And it is on this line that we propose to fight our battle for the ballot – all peaceably, but nevertheless persistently through to complete triumph, when all United States citizens shall be recognised as equals before the law."

Anthony's lecture tour plainly worried her prosecutor, U. S. Attorney Richard Crowley. In a letter to Senator Benjamin F. Butler, Anthony wrote, "I have just closed a canvass of this county from which my jurors are to be drawn and I rather guess the U. S. District Attorney who is very bitter will hardly find twelve men so ignorant on the citizen's rights as to agree on a verdict of guilty. In May, however, Crowley convinced Judge Ward Hunt (the recently appointed justice of the U. S. Supreme Court who would hear Anthony's case) that Anthony had prejudiced potential jurors, and Hunt agreed to move the trial out of Monroe County to Canandaigua in Ontario County. Hunt set a new opening date for the trial of June 17.

Anthony responded to the judge's move by immediately launching a lecture tour in Ontario County. Anthony spoke for twenty-one days in a row, finally concluding her tour in Canandaigua, the county seat, on the night before the opening of her trial.

Trial

Going into the June trial, Anthony and her lawyers were somewhat less optimistic about the outcome than they had been a few months before. In April, the U. S. Supreme Court handed down its first two major interpretations of the recently enacted Civil War Amendments, rejected the claimed violations in both cases and construing key provisions narrowly. Of special concern to Anthony was the Court's decision in *Bradwell vs. Illinois*, where the Court had narrowly interpreted the Fourteenth Amendment's equal protection clause to uphold a state law that prohibited women from becoming lawyers. In an April 27 letter, Anthony anxiously sought out Benjamin Butler's views of the decision, noting that the whole Democratic press was jubilant over the infamous interpretation of the amendments."

Even without the Supreme Court's narrow interpretation of the amendments, many observers expressed skepticism about the strength of Anthony's case. An editorial in the New York Times concluded:

"Miss Anthony is not in the remotest degree likely to gain her case, nor if it were ever so desirable that women should vote, would hers be a good case. When so important a change in our Constitution as she proposes is made, it will be done openly and unmistakably, and not left to the subtle interpretation of a clause adopted for a wholly different purpose."

In a lengthy response to the *Times* editorial, Elizabeth Cady Stanton quoted Judge Selden as confidently telling Anthony, "There is law enough not only to protect you in the exercise of your right to vote, but to enfranchise every woman in the land."

On June 17, 1873, Anthony, wearing a new bonnet faced with blue silk and draped with a veil, walked up the steps of the Canandaigua courthouse on the opening day of her trial. The second-floor courtroom was filled to capacity. The spectators included a former president, Millard Fillmore, who had travelled over from Buffalo, where he practiced law. Judge Ward Hunt sat behind the bench, looking stolid in his black broadcloth and neck wound in a white neckcloth. Anthony described Hunt as a small-brained, pale-faced, prim-looking man, enveloped in a faultless black suit and a snowy white tie.

Richard Crowley made the opening statement for the prosecution:

"We think, on the part of the Government, that there is no question about it either one way or the other, neither a question of fact, nor a question of law, and that whatever Miss Anthony's intentions may have been – whether they were good or otherwise, she did not have a right to vote upon that question, and if she did vote without having a lawful right to vote, then there is no question but what she is guilty of violating a law of the United States in that behalf enacted by the Congress of the United States."

The prosecution's chief witness was Beverly W. Jones, a twenty-five-year-old inspector of elections. Jones testified that he witnessed Anthony cast a ballot on November 5 in Rochester's Eighth Ward. Jones added he accepted Anthony's completed ballot and placed it a ballot box. On cross-examination, Selden asked Jones if he had also been present when Anthony registered four days earlier, and whether objections to Anthony's registration had not been considered and rejected at that time. Jones agreed that was the case, and that Anthony's name had been added to the voting rolls.

The main factual argument that the defence hoped to present was that Anthony reasonably believed that she was entitled to vote, and therefore could not be guilty of the crime of "knowingly" casting an illegal vote. To support this argument, Henry Selden called himself as a witness to testify:

"Before the last election, Miss Anthony called upon me for advice, upon the question whether she was or was not a legal voter. I examined the question, and gave her my opinion, unhesitatingly, that the laws and Constitution of the United States, authorised her to vote, as well as they authorise any man to vote."

Selden then called Anthony as a witness, so she might testify as to her vote and her state of mind on Election Day. District Attorney Crowley objected: "She is not a competent as a witness on her own behalf." Judge Hunt sustained the objection, barring Anthony from taking the stand. The defence rested.

The prosecution called to the stand John Pound, an Assistant United States Attorney who had attended a January examination in which Anthony testified about her registration and vote. Pound testified that Anthony testified at that time that she did not consult Selden until after registering to vote. Selden, after conferring with Anthony, agreed that their meeting took place immediately after her registration, rather than before as his own testimony had suggested. On cross-examination, Pound admitted that Anthony had testified at her examination that she had not a particle of doubt about her right as a citizen to vote. With Pound's dismissal from the stand, the evidence closed and the legal arguments began.

Selden opened his three-hour-long argument for Anthony by stressing that she was prosecuted purely on account of her gender:

"If the same act had been done by her brother under the same circumstances, the act would have been not only innocent, but honourable and laudable; but having been done by a woman it was said to be a crime. The crime therefore consists not in the act done, but in the simple fact that the person doing it was a woman and not a man, I believe this is the first instance in which a woman has been arraigned in a criminal court, merely on account of her sex."

Selden stressed that the vote was essential to women receiving fair treatment from legislatures: "Much has been done, but much more remains to be done by women. If they had possessed the elective franchise, the reforms which have cost them a quarter of a century of labour would have been accomplished in a year."

Central to Selden's argument that Anthony cast a legal vote was the recently enacted Fourteenth Amendment:

"It will be seen, therefore, that the whole subject, as to what should constitute the "privileges and immunities" of the citizen being left to the States, no question, such as we now present, could have arisen under the original constitution of the United States. But now, by the Fourteenth Amendment, the United States have not only declared what constitutes citizenship, both in the United States and in the several States, securing the rights of citizens to all persons born or naturalised in the United States; but have absolutely prohibited the States from making or enforcing any law which shall abridge the privileges or immunities of citizens of the United States. By virtue of this provision, I insist that the act of Miss Anthony in voting was lawful."

Finally, Selden insisted that even if the Fourteenth Amendment did not make Anthony's vote legal, she could not be prosecuted because she acted in the good faith belief that her vote *was* legal:

Miss Anthony believed, and was advised that she had a right to vote. She was also advised, as was clearly the fact, that the question as to her right could not be brought before the courts for trial, without her voting or offering to vote, and if either was criminal, the one was as much so as the other. Therefore she stands arraigned as a criminal, for taking the only steps by which it was possible to bring the great constitutional question as to her right, before the tribunals of the country for adjudication. If for thus acting, in the most perfect good faith, with motives as pure and impulses as noble as any which can find place in honour's breast in the administration of justice, she was by the laws of her country to be condemned as a criminal, she must abide the consequences. Her condemnation, however, under such circumstances, would only add another most weighty reason to those which Selden had already advanced, to show that women need the aid of the ballot for their protection.

After District Attorney Crowley offered his two-hour response for the prosecution, Judge Hunt drew from his pocket a paper and began reading an opinion that he had apparently prepared before the trial started. Hunt declared, "The Fourteenth Amendment gives no right to a woman to vote, and the voting by Miss Anthony was in violation of the law." The judge rejected Anthony's argument that her good faith precluded a finding that she "knowingly" cast an illegal vote: "Assuming that Miss Anthony believed she had a right to vote, that fact constitutes no defence if in truth she had not the right. She voluntarily gave a vote which was illegal, and thus is subject to the penalty of the law." Hunt that surprised Anthony and her attorney by directing a verdict of guilty: "Upon this evidence I suppose there is no question for the jury and that the jury should be directed to find a verdict of guilty."

In her diary that night Anthony angrily described the trial as the greatest judicial outrage history has ever recorded! "We were convicted before we had a hearing and the trial was a mere farce." During the entire trial, as Henry Selden pointed out, "No juror spoke a word during the trial, from the time they were impanelled to the time they were discharged." Had the jurors had an opportunity to speak, there was reason to believe that Anthony would not have been convicted. A newspaper quoted one juror as saying, "Could I have spoken, I should have answered 'not guilty,' and the men in the jury box would have sustained me."

Sentencing

The next day Selden argued for a new trial on the ground that Anthony's constitutional right to a trial by jury had been violated. Judge Hunt promptly denied the motion. Then, before sentencing,

Hunt asked, "Has the prisoner anything to say why sentence shall not be pronounced?" The exchange that followed stunned the crowd in the Canandaigua courthouse:

"Yes, your honour, I have many things to say; for in your ordered verdict of guilty, you have trampled under foot every vital principle of our government. My natural rights, my civil rights, my political rights, my judicial rights, are all alike ignored. Robbed of the fundamental privilege of citizenship, I am degraded from the status of a citizen to that of a subject; and not only myself individually, but all of my sex, are, by your honour's verdict, doomed to political subjection under this, so-called, form of government."

Judge Hunt interrupted, "The Court cannot listen to a rehearsal of arguments the prisoner's counsel has already consumed three hours in presenting."

But Anthony would not be deterred. She continued, "May it please your honour, I am not arguing the question, but simply stating the reasons why sentence cannot, in justice, be pronounced against me. Your denial of my citizen's right to vote, is the denial of my right of consent as one of the governed, the denial of my right of representation as one of the taxed, the denial of my right to a trial by a jury of my peers as an offender against law, therefore, the denial of my sacred rights to life, liberty, property."

"The Court cannot allow the prisoner to go on."

"But your honour will not deny me this one and only poor privilege of protest against this high-handed outrage upon my citizen's rights. May it please the Court to remember that since the day of my arrest last November, this is the first time that either myself or any person of my disfranchised class has been allowed a word of defence before judge or jury."

"The prisoner must sit down, the Court cannot allow it."

"All of my prosecutors, from the eighth ward corner grocery politician, who entered the compliant, to the United States Marshal, Commissioner, District Attorney, District Judge, your honour on the bench, not one is my peer, but each and all are my political sovereigns; and had your honour submitted my case to the jury, as was clearly your duty, even then I should have had just cause of protest, for not one of those men was my peer; but, native or foreign born, white or black, rich or poor, educated or ignorant, awake or asleep, sober or drunk, each and every man of them was my political superior; hence, in no sense, my peer. Even, under such circumstances, a commoner of England, tried before a jury of Lords, would have far less cause to complain than should I, a woman, tried before a jury of men. Even my counsel, the Hon. Henry R. Selden, who has argued my cause so ably, so earnestly, so unanswerably before your honour, is my political sovereign. Precisely as no disfranchised person is entitled to sit upon a jury, and no woman is entitled to the franchise, so, none but a regularly admitted lawyer is allowed to practice in the courts, and no woman can gain admission to the bar. Hence, jury, judge, counsel, must all be of the superior class.

"The Court must insist – the prisoner has been tried according to the established forms of law."

"Yes, your honour, but by forms of law all made by men, interpreted by men, administered by men, in favour of men, and against women; and hence, your honour's ordered verdict of guilty; against a United States citizen for the exercise of "that citizen's right to vote," simply because the citizen was a woman and not a man. But, yesterday, the same man made forms of law, declared it a crime punishable with $1,000 fine and six months imprisonment, for you, or me, to give a cup of cold water, a crust of bread, or a night's shelter to a panting fugitive as he was tracking his way to Canada. And every man or woman in whose veins coursed a drop of human sympathy violated that wicked law, reckless of consequences, and was justified in so doing. As then, the slaves who got their freedom must take it over, or under, or through the unjust forms of law, precisely so, now, must women, to get their right to a voice in this government, take it; and I have taken mine, and mean to take it at every possible opportunity."

"The Court orders the prisoner to sit down. It will not allow another word."

"When I was brought before your honour for trial, I hoped for a broad and liberal interpretation of the Constitution and its recent amendments, that should declare equality of rights the national guarantee to all persons born or naturalised in the United States. But failing to get this justice, even to get a trial by a jury not of my peers, I ask not leniency at your hands but rather the full rigors of the law."

"The Court must insist."

Finally, Anthony sat down, only to be immediately ordered by Judge Hunt to rise again. Hunt pronounced sentence: "The sentence of the Court is that you pay a fine of one hundred dollars and the costs of the prosecution."

Anthony protested. "May it please your honour, I shall never pay a dollar of your unjust penalty. All the stock in trade I possess is a $10,000 debt, incurred by publishing my paper, *The Revolution* four years ago, the sole object of which was to educate all women to do precisely as I have done, rebel against your manmade, unjust, unconstitutional forms of law, that tax, fine, imprison and hang women, while they deny them the right of representation in the government; and I shall work on with might and main to pay every dollar of that honest debt, but not a penny shall go to this unjust claim. And I shall earnestly and persistently continue to urge all women to the practical recognition of the old revolutionary maxim that resistance to tyranny is obedience to God."

Judge Hunt, in a move calculated to preclude any appeal to a higher court, ended the trial by announcing, "Madam, the Court will not order you committed until the fine is paid."

Epilogue

True to her word, Anthony never paid a penny of her fine. Her petition to Congress to remit the fine was never acted upon, but no serious effort was ever made by the government to collect.

Anthony tried to turn her trial and conviction into political gains for the women suffrage movement. She ordered 3,000 copies of the trial proceedings printed and distributed them to political activists, politicians, and libraries. In the eyes of some, the trial had elevated Anthony to the status of the martyr, while for others the effect may have been to diminish her status to that of a common criminal. Many in the press, however, saw Anthony as the ultimate victor. One New York paper observed, "If it is a mere question of who got the best of it, Miss Anthony is still ahead. She has voted and the American constitution has survived the shock. Fining her one hundred dollars does not rule out the fact that women voted, and went home, and the world jogged on as before."

Susan B Anthony

Born: Feb. 15, 1820, Adams, Mass., U.S.

Died: March 13, 1906, Rochester, N.Y.

U.S. pioneer in the women's suffrage movement.

A precocious child, she learned to read and write at the age of three. After attending a boarding school in Philadelphia, she took a teaching position in a Quaker seminary in upstate New York. She taught at a female academy (1846–49) and then settled in her family home near Rochester, N.Y. There she met many leading abolitionists, including Frederick Douglass and William Lloyd Garrison. The rebuff of her attempt to speak at a temperance meeting in Albany in 1852 prompted her to join Elizabeth Cady Stanton in organising the Woman's State Temperance Society of New York. From this time she was a tireless campaigner for abolition and women's rights. During the early phase of the Civil War she helped in organising the Women's National Loyal League, which urged the case for emancipation. After the war, she campaigned unsuccessfully to have the language of the Fourteenth Amendment altered to allow for woman as well as "Negro" suffrage. In 1868, she represented the Working Women's Association of New York, which she had recently organised, at the National Labor Union convention. In January 1869 she organised a woman suffrage convention in Washington, D.C., and in May she and Stanton formed the National Woman Suffrage Association (NWSA). As a test of the legality of the suffrage provision of the Fourteenth Amendment, she cast a vote in the 1872 presidential election in Rochester. She was arrested, convicted (the judge's directed verdict of guilty had been written before the trial began), and fined; though she refused to pay the fine, the case was carried no further. She served as president of the National American Woman Suffrage Association (1892–1900) and lectured throughout the country for a federal women's suffrage amendment.